ALSO BY **JOSHUA S. LEVY**:

The Jake Show

Finn and Ezra's Bar Mitzvah Time Loop

Joshua S. Levy

Katherine Tegen Books
An Imprint of HarperCollins Publishers

Katherine Tegen Books is an imprint of HarperCollins Publishers.

Finn and Ezra's Bar Mitzvah Time Loop
Copyright © 2024 by Joshua S. Levy
All rights reserved. Printed in the United States of America.
No part of this book may be used or reproduced in any manner whatsoever without written permission except in the case of brief quotations embodied in critical articles and reviews. For information address HarperCollins Children's Books, a division of HarperCollins Publishers, 195 Broadway, New York, NY 10007.
www.harpercollinschildrens.com

Library of Congress Control Number: 2023943334
ISBN 978-0-06-324824-3

Typography by Andrea Vandergrift
24 25 26 27 28 LBC 5 4 3 2 1
First Edition

For my family.
I'd get myself trapped in a loop with you anytime.

★ PROLOGUE ★

A door opens.
    It's been a long time (or is it no time at all?). But finally. *Finally*. Something *different* is happening. Something new. Some*one*.

My heart *thump thump thumps* in my chest, like the second hand of a clock on the last day of school. I reach for him—even though he's too far away to touch—stumble forward, face-plant onto the floor.

Questions swirl around me.

Voices close in.

My mom moves to help me up. My dad sprints toward us.

I try to shake them off, escape through the crowd, race against time to the mysterious figure before he disappears... before *everyone* disappears.

Before I have to do this all. over. again.

1

EZRA

My first bar mitzvah took forever.

Friday night dinner was even more of a disaster than usual. We hosted the meal at our house after shul, just our immediate family and a few of my best friends—and everything that could have gone wrong, did. Barely enough food. Tableside blowup between my dad and older sister, Avital. My mom, so upset that she left to take a walk in the rain.

Torah reading in shul the next morning started okay—until my five-year-old sister, Eliana, wandered over to me in the middle of the fourth aliyah and barfed onto my Shabbos shoes. I took a break to clean up but never really recovered. And when I eventually backed away from the bimah, relieved to be done, some random congregant coughed into his hand, pointed at me with his cane, and told me that I was "Nu, a little flat."

And then there was the Sunday party held at the Bergenville Hotel and Convention Center, Ballroom C. ("As in Chaim," my cheesy uncle joked.) So close to the New Jersey Turnpike that you could smell the exhaust from passing cars. Some gross food, mostly leftovers from shul lunch the day before. My friends, trying (and failing) to pump me up. And then my speech, which was . . . fine, considering I put zero effort into it. Not that it would have mattered either way. My parents didn't hear a word. My dad spent the whole thing hunched in a corner, faced away from me, busy yelling at Avital for whatever it was she did this time. And while my mom was technically within earshot, she spent the speech with her head flamingoed under our table, trying to pry my littlest sister Esty free from one of the legs.

According to the bar mitzvah invitations, this weekend was supposed to be about *me*. But I'm also the middle kid of five kids, so you do the math. I could have skipped the speech and recited the ABCs at the podium instead. They wouldn't have noticed. At least I was now thirteen, which meant that I was almost in high school, which meant that in only a few short years I could leave for yeshiva and not spend every waking moment being completely ignored. I was counting the seconds until my life could *finally* be about me.

Hence my approach to the weekend: Just get through it. Just get past it. I barely said a word at Friday night dinner. I sped-read the parsha like my life depended on it. And I spent most of the Sunday party stealing glances at the clock on the wall, counting the minutes until I could put this whole annoying thing behind me.

Speech over, I got a unanimous round of applause, bursts of "Mazel tov! Mazel tov!" from the crowd. So not a total loss. A little more dancing and the bar mitzvah would be over. One more box checked on the way to my *real* life.

I smiled, took another look at the clock, and—

My second bar mitzvah went *weird*, mostly because it happened again, same as the first. Friday night dinner. ("Avital, you need to have more respect!") Torah reading in shul on Shabbos day. ("Nu, a little flat!") Sunday party at the hotel, Ballroom C. ("As in Chaim!") I pushed away the panic. The only logical explanation was that I'd had a vivid, semi-prophetic dream on Thursday night.

I chalked it up to nerves and talked myself into believing everything was completely normal. My brain knew I'd been dreading the bar mitzvah. And it wasn't like the details were *that* hard to predict. Avital and our dad had been squabbling for weeks. Mr. Bendish—a cranky old man who complained in shul about *everything*—probably hadn't liked a Torah reading since 1975. And Uncle Chaim made terrible puns *all the time*.

The real miracle of the occasion would have been if my parents had remembered that, yes, they did have a kid named Ezra and, yes, it was his bar mitzvah this weekend. By lunchtime Sunday, I'd convinced myself that I was imagining things. Just the bar mitzvah jitters, ha ha. Perfectly natural. We ate our crusty food. I gave my big speech. The crowd chirped their chorus of "Mazel tov!"—and then I blinked, reset, and woke up in my bed on Friday morning, like the whole thing had never happened. Again.

My *third* bar mitzvah did not go great. Friday night dinner. ("AVITAL, YOU NEED TO HAVE MORE RESPECT!") Torah reading. ("NU, A LITTLE FLAT!") Sunday party, Ballroom C. ("AS IN CHAIM!") *Breathe, Ezra. Breathe.* I kept rapid-fire asking my parents and siblings what was happening, why they were playing this cruel joke on me, *if they were also reliving my bar mitzvah over and over.*

They were not.

"Are you sure you're okay?"

"Let's take your temperature."

"I think the stress must be getting to him, Yosef."

Every reaction *except* "Yes, of course we believe that you keep repeating this weekend and no one else seems to notice but you. How can we help?"

They weren't listening. They couldn't hear what I was trying to say. What else is new.

For the speech that time around, I really let them have it:

"What is *wrong* with you people?! Can't you see that something strange is going on?! Imma, Abba, you're supposed to take care of me! I know you've got *four* other kids to worry about and don't usually have the time for little old Ezra. But you'd think that on *my* weekend, you'd listen to me. You think I *like* this? You think I want to be stuck here with all of you?! I can't *wait* to get out of here. And another thing—!"

At least I finally got their attention for three whole minutes. My dad and Avital took a time-out from their argument to stare at me, mouths open, chins on the floor. My mom let Esty alone under the table, my shrieking louder than her cries. My older brother, Eitan, was standing in the back, motionless with horror, pitcher tilting out so much soda into his glass that it spilled over the top, waterfalling over the rim of the bar—like he was the one frozen in time and not me.

Five minutes in, Uncle Chaim gently tried to remove me from the stage. I threw him off, pressed my palms hard against my temples: "YOU ARE NOT FUNNY AND YOU HAVE NEVER BEEN FUNNY AND 'C, AS IN CHAIM' ISN'T EVEN REALLY A JOKE! IT'S JUST A LETTER AND YOUR NAME! THAT'S NOT ANYTHING! ANYTHING!" No one was safe. Not Mr. Bendish. Not my parents. Not my friends. I got *everything* off my chest. Roasted the lot of 'em. What did it matter anyway? They wouldn't remember a thing.

Sure enough, the clock struck 1:36 p.m., and it happened again. And again. And again.

So welcome. Take a seat. Thank you for coming. Today, I am a man. And also yesterday. And tomorrow too. What's the difference? Who's got the energy to be mad about things that never change? I've spent most of the last dozen bar mitzvahs in a fog. Going through the motions. Mouthing along to words I know are just around the corner.

Always: "Avital, you need to have more respect."
Always: "Nu, a little flat."
Always: "Ballroom C, as in Chaim."

Always on Friday night, Eitan steps on Eliana's LEGO mess and breaks the skin on the bottom of his foot. Always on Saturday night, Avital sneaks my dad's car without telling him, caught in the act when she gets back home. Always right before the Sunday speech, my mother ruffles my hair and says, "It's not every day our baby boy has a bar mitzvah."

Now *that's* a funny joke.

This has got to be—what?—the fifteenth time around? Twentieth?

I stand and shuffle to the front of the crowd. There's my dad, right on cue, cornering Avital ("No respect." "No respect." "No respect.") for last night. Here's my mom: "It's not every day our baby boy has a bar mitzvah." Esty squirms to the floor and starts to cry, clutching a table leg for dear life.

"This week's parsha," I start, my voice dull (and "Nu, a little flat." "Nu, a little flat." "Nu, a little flat."). I recite the words and stare at some spot on the opposite wall, my eyes glazed over.

Ballroom C ("As in Chaim." "As in Chaim." "As in Chaim.") is like all the other ballrooms on this side of the hotel: just a section of a larger room, divided into thirds via fake walls. I'm up on a raised dais, facing a small dance floor whose scuff patterns I know like the back of my hand and a dozen circular tables filled with friends and family who are not *nearly* as tired of this day as I am. I glance at the clock on the wall: 1:30 p.m.

Almost over.

Never over.

Make it stop.

And then a door opens. Across the ballroom, a kid wanders in, silhouetted by sunlight beaming in through nearby windows. Once through, he sticks out like a sore thumb. His clothes, for one thing. Jeans and a hoodie. No yarmulke. Mostly, though, I notice him not because of what he's wearing—but because he's here at all.

Someone new.

I trip off the stage.

"Is everything all right?"

"Give him some space."

"Do you need water?"

I ignore them. Begin to run. But halfway across the room, I trip again, fall to my knees, raise my eyes back to the clock. It's too late.

The kid is still watching, still staring, now holding up a handwritten sign in the back of the room. Sharpie cap in his mouth, a smile blooms at the edges of his eyes. The poster board reads:

I KNOW YOUR SECRET. MEET ME YESTERDAY.

And then it's 1:36 p.m. and I'm back to the start.

2

FINN

"He'll be here."

"We know, buddy," my dad says from across the table.

My mom rakes cold eggs from one side of her plate to the other. "Happy to hang out here together as long as you want."

We sit in silence for another few minutes. The waiter comes around to refill my parents' tea, again. The hotel guests next to us stand up; their table gets cleaned, and another family is seated *again*. It's more crowded now than when we got here. The "lunch rush," as our waiter has mentioned like ten times. At one point, he calls over some guy from behind the hotel front desk. The concierge marches over—chin up, nostrils wide—to ask, "Is there anything I can do for you?" in a tone of voice that says, "Is there anything I can do to make you leave?"

Getting the hint, my dad checks the time on his phone. "Should we at least get the bill?" he asks my mom.

She clears her throat and gives my hand a quick squeeze. "I have nowhere to be but here," Mom says, before waving the front desk guy away and ordering another round of tea.

If Too-Perfect Dad of the Year over here is feeling antsy, you know we've been sitting for a while. "Who's supposed to be meeting us again?" he asks.

"I told you," I say. "My friend."

Mom and Dad share a glance.

"I have friends, you know."

Mom gives my hand another pat. "Of course, sweetie, we know. For sure."

Dad lifts his mug into the air, like he's making a toast to the chalkboard specials on the wall. "And no matter what, *we* love you."

Brutal, guys. Savage.

Parents. Can't live with 'em, can't be trapped in a fifty-five-hour time loop without 'em, amirite?

Not that there aren't *some* advantages to being stuck inside an unexplained temporal anomaly. Unlimited ice cream for one thing. Inhale a whole carton of mint chocolate chip when the timeline is moving *straight*? Stomachache city. Inhale it before a loop resets? You'll wake up three days ago, feeling fantastic, plenty of room for breakfast.

Then there's the practice-makes-perfect element. Run any single weekend long enough, you'll pick up all the tricks. Take school, for example. At *precisely* 9:07 a.m., the school custodian will accidentally leave the door to the AV room unlocked. If you make it inside (ducked low, lights off) before he remembers and returns to lock up at 9:13, you can watch TV by yourself all day. No one will notice. Pull the fire alarm any time *after* 11:23:56 (and not a second before), they'll cancel PE. (But do it between 12:08 and 12:25, you'll also get caught.) Alas—unless you skip school entirely—there doesn't seem to be a way out of Ms. Bethe's weekly vocab quiz. She runs a tight ship, even for a semi-omniscient, time-traveling wanderer such as myself.

I know, I know. Skip school?! But, Finn, you *love* school, guy. True true. Do good in middle school so you can get into the best high school so you can get into the best college so you can get the best job so you can *finally* move out and force your mom and dad to be obsessed with something else for a change. And school's the ticket. Usually, it's head down, nose to the grindstone. But *you* try defining "rudimentary" and "nonplussed" over and over (and over). How many different sentences can a person even make with the word "antediluvian"? (One loop, I tanked the whole thing on purpose. Wrote things like: "My auntie Diluvian made us blueberry pancakes for breakfast." Got a 0/10 on the quiz, and my parents still insisted on pinning it to the fridge like some medal on a war hero's chest, convinced that I "should have at least gotten extra credit for creativity! Let's call your teacher!")

Here's what I've worked out, choose-your-own-adventure style: When the alarm goes off on Loop-Friday morning, if I shout, "Ugh! I don't want to go to school today!"—my mom will not, in fact, let me stay home. She will instead burst into my room and swipe the curtains wide in a "Rise and shine, Your Majesty!" kind of way. And if I groan loud enough, she will actually say, "Rise and shine, Your Majesty!"

Pretending to be sick is also a no-go. If I don't put my heart into it, my parents don't believe me. And if I *do* give it everything I've got—bolt from the bed, sprint down the hall, steal the heating pad, warm up my forehead, hack the thermometer, sprinkle water on my sheets, throw crumpled tissues around the room, cough cough sneeze sneeze, "Oh, I'm so achy, boo-hoo, meh"—my dad panic-schedules a pediatrician appointment first thing and then I'm stuck at Dr. Bread's office for like three hours, which is *such* a waste of time, even though technically I have unlimited time.

Better to keep things simple. Saying these exact magic words, in this exact order: "Please, Mom. I'm feeling a little anxious about the bar mitzvah this weekend. Would you mind if I took the day for myself?"

Breathe in . . . hold it . . . hold it . . . *loooong siiiigh.*

That gets me out of school for the day every time, no Dr. Bread. I've also workshopped a few useful variants. If I stretch out the sigh for an extra 2.5 seconds, she'll let me go back to bed for half an hour, no questions asked. And if I replace "if I took the day for myself" with "if we spent the day together," her face will light up, she'll run to tell the story to my dad, and he'll whip up stacks of blueberry pancakes for breakfast (just like Auntie Diluvian), "because we love you, Finn," insisting that my mom rest on the couch while he "cooks up a big family breakfast!" They're a bit like video game characters that way. But instead of figuring out that Up-Up-Down-A-B gets you a rocket boost or whatever, I learned that admiring my dad's new skillet (three compliments minimum) unlocks a bonus round of pancakes, banana chocolate chip. After a while, parents are kind of predictable NPCs.

Which is good, because I *really* need them off my back.

Yesterday: Friday morning.

Blerk. Blerk. Blerk.

I slapped my alarm and ran the standard play: "Please, Mom. I'm feeling a little anxious about the bar mitzvah this weekend. Would you mind if I took the day for myself?" Jumbo sigh.

But I didn't go back to bed. I needed as much time alone as possible, which is harder than it should be. It doesn't matter what I say or what I do. Pancakes, no pancakes. The loops have *rules*, immovable laws of nature: I can't ever make it past 1:36 p.m. on Sunday. I can't leave myself notes for the next go-round. And if I don't wind up at school or with the doctor on Loop-Friday, my parents will eventually barge in, announce that they've *both* called in sick to work, and—literal tears in their eyes—insist we spend every waking moment together until dinner.

"A special family day." —Loop Dad, Variant Six.

"The three musketeers!" —Loop Mom, Variants Three and Seven.

"We love you so much, kiddo!" —Both Loop Parents, *all* variants.

Time loop or no time loop, my parents love me . . . a little too much. And there is apparently no timeline in the vast multiverse where they're willing to just lay off me for once.

I only get thirty minutes before they come to give me the "Isn't it wonderful!" news that we'll be attached at the hip until sundown. This loop, I used the free time to consolidate my research, prep for the big meetup, and write down everything I know about *the other kid*. The kid I'm positive is stuck in the loop with me.

Name: Ezra Akiva Rosen
Age: 13 (Today)
Parents: Hodaya and Yosef Rosen
Siblings: Esty (9 months), Eliana (5), Eitan (15), and Avital (18)

That intro carefully bulleted onto the page, I scrawled out the remaining intel in one long paragraph that Ms. Bethe would hate: How I first noticed Ezra on the third or fourth loop. It was early days still. I was wandering around our end of the Bergenville Hotel, sad and scared, trying to think. My Sunday bar mitzvah party is (was, will be) in the Bergenville. Nothing fancy. Appetizers defrosted from the box (mini hot dogs, mozzarella sticks, egg rolls). A "DJ" (just my uncle Toby and his unpaid Spotify account). And some classmates who never actually talk to me at school, handing me cards their parents obviously wrote for them, awkwardly bopping around to whatever Toby found by searching the internet for "Songs kids like."

ANYWAY. The Bergenville. My bar mitzvah party is in Ballroom A. An event I was not looking forward to, even when I thought I'd only have to live through it the one time. It's just, you try inviting everyone you've ever known to what everyone else says is the most important weekend of your life, spending week after week being all like, "So are you coming to my bar mitzvah?" "Hey, you never returned your invitation" and "No big deal. My parents are trying to get a head count"—while half expecting a bad turnout but still hoping for something else, all for there to be like five kids in the whole place plus family you never even see plus your parents working the room as *the worst* party-hype people in recorded history and even then everyone leaves early and your uncle goes, *out loud*, "Is this all your friends, Finn?"

And then you run that exact thing *over and over and over again*.

So yeah. A few loops in, I stretched my time-loop wings, snuck Toby five bucks to play Elton John's "Your

Song" (cheat code for getting my parents to freaking leave me alone for like five minutes), and stole away to wander the halls.

The Bergenville complex is huge. The hotel proper—two towers of fifteen stories, a lobby restaurant, and lots of small ballrooms—is connected to some larger businessy conference center across an aboveground walkway. In our little corner of the hotel universe, there's Ballroom A (my bar mitzvah), Ballroom B (empty), and Ballroom C. It was hard to miss what was going on through the door down the hall, what with all the echoes of "Mazel tov!" and chair lifting and whatnot. Ezra's party looked nothing like mine. Lots of yarmulkes and Jewish music. But two bar mitzvahs in the same hotel? Seeing him for the first time was a shock. The possibilities hit me like a ton of bricks. It couldn't be a coincidence.

Or maybe it could.

But what else did I have to do? I've got all the time in the world. Hence me dedicating these most recent loops to one thing: Ezra Rosen. Spying on him. Trailing his family. Gathering data. Most of it's useless, like how Eitan is trying out for his school's basketball team or how Eliana can "count to a thousand, wanna see?" (I usually don't, and also she can't.) But some of it... some of it's changed *everything*.

Like mine, Ezra's family behaves basically the same, every loop. Sure, you can talk them into playing out all sorts of scenarios. Same with my mom and dad. But *you've* got to trigger a change, and then they just . . . follow the path. It's like dropping a ball down different sides of a hill. The ball won't roll the same every time, but still, all it does is *roll*, you know?

Ezra though. Ezra's like me. Take Loop-Sunday for example. He'll go along with the circle dancing, the eating, that nonsense speech of his. But I've also seen him go off script.

Even then, I wasn't *sure*. Not right away. Not until I caught him lip-synching too. Because sometimes, also like me, he says everyone else's lines under his breath, like he's singing along to a favorite song. Except—no, that's not quite right. That's not how it feels. It's not singing along to a *favorite* song. It's singing along to a song you *hate* but cannot get out of your head no matter what you do, no matter how hard you try.

There's only one inescapable, impossible conclusion: Ezra Rosen is stuck in a time loop, just like me. So I watched and planned and, finally, put things into motion. Last go-round, I made contact and, this loop, I hacked my parents into driving me to the Bergenville a day early, on Loop-*Saturday*, even though the bar mitzvah parties aren't until Loop-Sunday. I figure this'll give us the space we need to conduct our business, no distractions. In retrospect, I probably should have given Ezra an exact time to meet me here. Funny how that detail didn't occur to me. But whatever. He'll understand. I'll wait here as long as it takes. That jerk front desk guy will be fine. My parents have nowhere to be. And once Ezra arrives, we'll finally figure out how to break free, how to move forward, together.

★ 3 ★

EZRA

The problem with mystery kid asking for a meetup at the hotel *yesterday* is that *yesterday* is Saturday. Saturday is Shabbos. And no one in my family drives from sundown Friday until sundown Saturday.

Good thing they don't care about me, then.

I did try to see if *anyone* wanted to join me for the long walk. It's about two hours to the hotel—across my neighborhood, through our borough's little downtown—two hours back. But my parents thought I was kidding, and my siblings laughed in my face *as if* I was kidding—at least proving that, just because one thing changes, doesn't mean anything else is going to change.

As soon as I'm done with Torah reading ("*You're* a

little flat," I tell Mr. Bendish on my way out), I ditch my black hat and jacket in my father's shtender and leave shul alone. They *might* notice I'm missing at the lunch *for my own bar mitzvah*. But they probably won't. Just in case, I left an excuse with Eitan and Avital, something about how "I need to go to my friend Shai's house, be back tonight." Nothing fancy. My parents will buy basically any excuse. And if not, who cares. Everything resets on Sunday anyway.

Covered in sweat, sleeves rolled up to my elbows, shirt untucked with tzitzis flying—I make it to the hotel and push against the manual revolving door. The familiar lobby isn't empty or full: A few businesspeople in suits standing by the elevator, chatting low. Some kids watching an iPad from a couch, while their parents tip a luggage attendant. A few teenagers up in the mezzanine café, giggling over a plate of muffins.

No better idea, I approach the front desk and crane my neck toward a tall concierge, name tag: "Andy Pauli."

I wait. Nothing. Tap his little bell. No response. And here I thought I was only invisible to my family.

"The main conference entrance is accessible from the other side of the hotel," he finally says, without looking away from his computer.

"Um, I'm not here for a conference," I say, no idea

what he's talking about. "I have my bar mitzvah in Ballroom C on Sunday? And um—" And *what*? Has he seen someone who may or may not have magic time powers? Did you happen to catch a glimpse of the kid—about my age, yea tall, sweatshirt—who was here *tomorrow*?

What was I thinking? Trekking all this way because someone I've never seen before held up a sign?

"Sorry," I say to the concierge. "Never mind."

"Excellent," he replies.

Then someone shouts at me from across the lobby: "Hey! Ezra!"

Startled to hear my name, I whiplash around. He's here. The kid. Inside the hotel restaurant, hopping up and down, waving at me like we're old friends.

"Everything okay, buddy?" a man says, emerging from the restaurant over the kid's right shoulder.

"And who's this?" a woman asks, hovering over his left.

They cross the lobby and join me at the front desk, where the rude concierge snorts for some reason and says, "I trust you enjoyed your"—he makes a big show of looking at his watch, nearly 2:00 p.m.—"*breakfast*." Then he turns and marches away on a dime. "If you'll excuse me."

"Dad, Mom," the kid says, ignoring the concierge,

"this is Ezra. My *friend*, see? His bar mitzvah is also at the Bergenville tomorrow."

As I walk forward, I take in the resemblances. They're all on the shorter side. Like his dad, the kid's got glasses, brown hair, and a pretty extreme widow's peak. Like his mom, he's got green eyes—although a bit brighter—a smattering of freckles, and a kind-of shoulder slouch that makes him look like he's leaning in close to hear what you've got to say.

The kid's parents look me up and down. I feel their gaze catch on my yarmulke, snag on my tzitzis. Can hear them thinking: *You don't seem like someone who's friends with our son.*

The dad smiles anyway. "Very nice to meet you."

Before I can reply, the kid rolls his eyes and says, "Uch, Dad. Can you give us some space, please? Ezra and I have very important matters to discuss."

"Very important matters, huh?" the dad asks. "Well, don't let us interfere."

The mom ruffles the kid's hair. "We'll be right over there, sweetie," she says, motioning to the café at the top of the stairs. The kid's parents cover him in hugs and kisses like they're dropping him off at an international airport and not walking fifteen steps to grab a coffee.

"Elevator is this way," the dad says to the mom, and the two head off, arm in arm.

"Finn," the kid says, sticking his hand out as soon as his parents are gone. "Sorry about them."

"No problem," I say, still not understanding any of this. Who this person is. Why I'm here. "I'm Ezra—"

"Ezra Akiva Rosen," Finn finishes for me. "I was worried you weren't gonna make it."

"Sorry. I keep Shabbos and had to walk."

"Walk!" Finn slaps his forehead. "Shoot. I knew that. I'm really sorry. And I'm double-triple-extra sorry I didn't give you a specific time. I've only had them bring me here twice before on Loop-Saturday. It's not yet an exact science. Practice makes perfect and all that. But you get it."

I do not.

Finn points toward the restaurant. "Lunch? I've been eating for like four hours straight, but we can order something if you want. My parents will totally pay for it."

"No, thanks," I say, scanning the menu display. "I keep kosher too."

Finn cringes. "Ugh. Sorry. Of course. I swear, I'm not doing this on purpose. You do you."

"It's fine."

Finn smirks. "Hang in the lobby, then? Come up with the plan?"

We sit down on one of the couches and Finn just... stares at me, crossing and uncrossing his legs, tapping his fingers. In the span of ten seconds—with all the fidgeting—Finn's glasses fall down his nose approximately ten thousand times. Half a minute in, he starts fast-drumming on the pillows so loud that it summons the concierge, who hisses at us to "quiet down or leave."

"Sorry," Finn says, stopping the drumbeat, sitting on his hands. The concierge disappears again, and Finn finally blurts out, "Well?! Don't leave me hanging! Tell me what you've tried!"

"Tried?"

"Yeah. You know, to get out."

"Get out."

"Don't tell me I'm wrong about you," Finn says. "No—what am I saying? I'm not wrong. You're *here*. Which means you saw me last loop and changed your behavior in this one. Which means I'm right. We're the same."

Understanding hits me like a wave. "The same?" I ask, barely a whisper.

Finn smiles. "Reliving these three days, over and over."

I can't help it. My brain explodes with relief. I leap across the couch and grab Finn in a bear hug. I'm not alone. And more than that: It's like I've been shouting this thing as loud as I can—"I'm stuck! Let me out!"—and somehow haven't made a sound. But finally, someone *hears me*.

Finn pats my back, and I withdraw to my side of the couch, wiping my cheeks. "Sorry."

He waves a hand. "Nah. I totes get it. But you're not alone anymore. *I'm* not alone anymore. We're in this together for some reason. And we're gonna get out together too."

Every sentence from this kid is better than the last. Maybe he really does have magic time powers.

"You know how to do that?" I ask. "Get out? Get to *Monday*?"

Finn laces his fingers behind his head. "Sweet, sweet Monday," he says dreamily. Then he gets serious. "Alas, I've tried everything I can think of. That's why I want to know what *you've* tried. Workshop what we might be missing."

"I . . . I haven't tried anything," I confess, suddenly embarrassed. "I mean, I have no idea what I *would* try, you know? How do you escape something you've never even heard of?"

Finn tilts his head to the side. "You've never heard of a time loop? Like, at all?"

"Should I have? Is this something that happens to people?"

Finn pinches the bridge of his nose like *I'm* the one who makes no sense. He sighs and pulls a pen and some folded pieces of paper from his pocket. The top page is titled "EVERYTHING I KNOW ABOUT EZRA AKIVA ROSEN." It contains endless teeny-tiny details of my life, handwritten front and back: Favorite foods . . . Siblings' birthdays . . . Grades?

"You . . . ," I start. "You've been watching me?"

Finn's face is suddenly panicked. And yeah, this is getting weird. Or, weird*er*.

"It's not what you think," he says.

I try to put the pieces together. "You . . . haven't secretly been following me and my family around, studying us like some kind of science project, all to figure out if I was stuck in a—what'd you call it? a *time loop*?—just like you?"

Finn blows air into his cheeks, holds it for a second, exhales. "Okay, so it's exactly what you think. Don't be mad?"

And, well, I'm not mad. Honestly, I wish he'd found me sooner. I wouldn't have minded a few less "loops" thinking I'd completely lost it.

"It's okay," I say, realizing something else. "Wait, you can keep notes from one . . . loop to the next?"

"A very good question, Mr. Rosen," Finn says, like he's my teacher or something. "But sorry, no. This is just what I remember from previous reconnaissance. Jotted it all down when I woke up yesterday morning." His eyes go wide. "Wait, can *you* keep stuff?"

I shake my head. "No. I've tried everything. Post-it notes on the fridge. Tally notches on the tree in front of our house. Quarters in the tzedakah box. It all resets on Sunday, one thirty-six p.m."

Finn chuckles to himself.

"What?" I ask.

He shrugs. "It's cute that you think that's *trying everything*."

I'm not entirely sure whether to be insulted. But Finn clearly knows a lot about a lot. I give him a pass.

"Well," I say, "what have *you* tried?"

"To overcome what I like to call the Preservation Conundrum?" He taps his chin a few times. "Let's see, let's see. Off the top of my head . . . I wrote my name in wet cement on multiple floors of an unfinished apartment building. I used my parents' credit card to run an online ad in one hundred and fifty-seven countries. It had my face and the words 'Remember Me!' flashing on the screen. Oh! And I sent a clock to myself on a FedEx route going against the rotation of Earth fast enough that the time zone of the plane was safely behind the reset point for three hours *after* Sunday at one thirty-six p.m."

I have so many questions, starting with: "Why'd you send a clock?"

Finn shrugs again. "Thematic consistency?" He shoves my biography page back into his pocket and holds up another piece of paper. "But now we're getting into the weeds when I think we need to take it from the top, yeah? Time Loops 101."

There's something written on one side of this new page. But Finn flips it to the back and lays it horizontal on the cushion between us. He clicks his pen and draws a line across the length of the page, straight along the middle.

"This is the past," Finn says, drawing an arrow at one end of the line and writing "PAST." "That's where we were before all this started.

"This is the future." He draws a second arrow at the opposite end and labels it. "That's where we want to go.

"Most people travel through time in a single direction." Finn draws a second line across the page, left to right. "Past to future. It's a one-way trip. Me and you, though?"

He starts a third line underneath the first two, past to future. But this time, when he gets to the middle, he slowly curls the pen upward and around, away from "FUTURE," back toward "PAST." He makes a single curl, a circle. Then he swirls his pen again and again and again. The third line never gets to "FUTURE."

"This is us," Finn explains. "Caught in a *time loop*. Experiencing the same weekend again and again. Some-*one* or some*thing* kicked us off course, dislodged us from the conventional flow of time. And now we're stuck here, until we can figure out how to fix the glitch and point ourselves back to the future."

Finn smiles. "Okay. I swear I didn't plan the reference."

"What reference?" I ask. A look of deep disappointment crosses Finn's face. I push past another flash of embarrassment. "And who *are* you? How do you know all this stuff?"

Finn straightens his back and puffs out his chest. "My name is Finn Julius Einstein, and I have watched a lot of movies."

I nod. "Ah, we don't have a TV at home."

Finn is again staring at me like getting caught in

a time loop is *not* the strangest thing he's ever experienced. "Not even Netflix?" he asks.

"Not even."

"Disney Plus?"

"Still no, although my brother Eitan's allowed to watch sports on his phone sometimes."

Finn breathes in deep and lets it out over four long seconds.

"This is going to be harder than I thought," he says. "Good thing I came prepared." He lifts the piece of paper from the couch and flips it over, clicking his pen a few times, licking the tip for no reason. "I made a checklist. I'm going to ask you a few questions, and we'll take it from there, okay?"

"Okay."

Finn pushes his glasses up the bridge of his nose and begins. "Have you run a perfect loop?"

A moment goes by. "Is that a question?"

Finn rubs his temples like I'm giving him a headache. "I'll explain: According to all stories ever about time loops, there's a few common ways out. One of the *most* common is the perfect loop. Helping people out. Solving problems. It's a whole . . . self-improvement thing. Almost always does the trick. I've tried running a perfect loop myself. Aced Ms. Bethe's quiz and brought in her favorite kind of apple. Caught the family of mice living in classroom four and released them into the wild. Made my parents breakfast in bed all three days. I even convinced Miles Richter that he *could* sing onstage in front of the whole school for the annual talent show if only he just *believed*."

A slideshow of memories runs through my head. Eitan yelping at the sharp LEGO gems on the floor. My mom wrestling Esty under the table. My dad fighting with Avital over the car. Me not helping with any of it.

"No," I say. "I've not done a perfect loop."

Finn makes an "X" next to the first bullet on his page.

"Have you discovered the true meaning of bar mitzvah?" he asks next, without looking up.

I consider asking him what that could possibly mean but think twice. "No."

"Ever been to the Bermuda Triangle?"

"No."

"Roswell, New Mexico?"

"Nope."

"To your knowledge, have you recently fallen into a wormhole and/or a shimmering rainbow portal of any kind?"

"Definitely not."

"Did you accidentally express a vaguely worded desire to a genie-trickster in some kind of monkey's paw situation?"

"*Huh?*"

"Maybe something like, 'I sure wish I had more time.' Open to multiple interpretations."

I silently stare long enough for him to go, "Let's assume not. Moving on. Almost done." He checks his paper again, clicks his pen a few more times. "I feel like I know the answer here already, but we've got to be thorough: Do you have a lost love in dire need of rescue and/or reconciliation?"

I laugh, but quiet when Finn's face tells me he's totally serious. "Um, also no."

"Can't be too careful," Finn says, looking down at the page. "Last one. It's a little dark, but I've got to ask. Are you now or have you ever been in contact with a person who will bring on the future apocalypse if he isn't stopped in the present, including but not limited to yourself and/or any children or grandchildren you may eventually have?"

"I . . . I'm not sure I get that one either." I pause, at least some of those words sinking in. "My own kids?!"

Finn tilts his head back and forth, weighing whether

to explain. "Let's put down . . . 'TBD.'" He folds up the checklist. "Good start though. We've got plenty of work to do."

"We do?"

"Absolutely. We're connected in some way. Both stuck in the loop. Both having a bar mitzvah on the same weekend in the same hotel. That can't be a coincidence. And seeing as *I've* already tried running a perfect loop, we know exactly where to start."

Finn goes quiet as I work out what he's trying to say. "You want to . . . come to my bar mitzvah? Be with me for *my* loop?"

I picture having to explain to my parents why this jumpy kid they've never seen before is suddenly following me around everywhere with a pen and paper. Then I remember they won't even notice.

"Why not?" Finn says, bouncing on the couch cushions, fake-boxing the air. I back up to avoid getting punched in the face. "We can sort it out together. Analyze the data and get you the most perfect loop possible. I bet that does it. We map things out for you. Then, when we're ready, we run two perfect loops simultaneously. Of course! That must be it. I help you, you help me. Responsibility. Kindness. Collaboration. The true meaning of bar mitzvah!" He stops moving, sits serious and still. "I'm *one hundred percent* sure. This has got to be the answer."

"It does?"

"Come on," Finn says. "When have I ever steered you wrong?"

"We just met five minutes ago," I point out.

He smiles. "Time flies when you're having fun."

4

FINN

The way I see it, the quest for Ezra's perfect loop has three stages: school, family, bar mitzvah.

The first bit should be easy. The guy is totally checked out at school, but school happens to be my specialty. So that one's in the bag.

The second piece is more complicated. There's a lot of them Rosens, and everyone's upset at someone. The dad at Avital (for basically everything). The mom at the dad (for being mad at Avital). Avital at Eitan (for not sticking up for her more). Even Eliana and Esty are always going at it (mostly over this three-story LEGO "superhero unicorn castle" that Eliana built and that Esty wants to eat).

And then there's the main event. Loop-*Saturday*,

and the mountain of bar mitzvah'ing Ezra has to climb. Lead prayers for his synagogue. Make a bunch of blessings. Read his *entire* Torah portion. Don't get me wrong, I do *some* of those things. My family belongs to Temple Rodeph Ahava, although it's been mostly a High Holidays deal until recently. Rosh Hashanah shofar blowing. Yom Kippur hangry praying. But we started going on Shabbat a few months ago, pre-loop. The rabbi there taught me to chant my haftorah, and I'm decent. But if I've got a little ditty to perform on Loop-Saturday, Ezra's starring in a three-act, one-man show.

Lots to do, lots to do.

And no time like the present.

Not wanting to freak out Ezra any more than necessary, I pretend that I *haven't* snuck into his school before. I'm all like, "What's the name of it? And how do you get there?"—even though I've scouted out Yeshivat Bnei Torah half a dozen times already, located off Route 701 in Saddle Creek. The YBT campus is small. Just a parking lot surrounding an industrial gray building. Playground and field off to the side. It's all elementary and middle school boys, who spend nine (*nine!*) hours in the building nearly every day, half on Judaic studies, half on the usual stuff—math, English, STEM, whatever. Thankfully, it's

Loop-*Friday*, and they let out early for Shabbat. But still. That's a lot of loop to perfect.

"Um, hi?" Ezra says as I sidle in next to him during morning prayers.

He's one of a few kids with a small black box hanging off his upper left arm, another attached to his forehead. Tefillin, I know they're called, from my previous trips to YBT. The boxes are square, each half the size of a standard Rubik's Cube. They're attached to leather straps, shiny black on one side, rough and brown on the other. The straps loop around Ezra's left arm—bicep to palm to middle finger—and fall along the sides of his head, from the back of his neck, over his shoulders, down to his waist. Not gonna lie, it's not *not* a weird look. But when I plop down in his row, *he* scans *me* from top to bottom, like I'm the one out of place.

"I don't . . . How'd you get in?" he whispers.

He means: How'd I get past the street-side metal gate and two security guards and locked front doors that can only be opened from the inside.

"I've got my ways," I say, not knowing how he'd take the whole story.

One loop was all it took to nail the dress code— black velvet yarmulke, white polo shirt, navy pants. And

I needed only a couple more loops to sort out the rest: How there's a kid from Riverdale named Binny Bloch whose family is moving to Fair Lawn in July who was supposed to try out YBT for the day and is on a pre-approved guest list but whose parents don't ask too many questions if you call them up first thing on Loop-Friday "on behalf of the Yeshivat Bnei Torah administration to apologize for the mix-up, you see, because we're all full today and are short-staffed but will call you to schedule the visit early next week, thank you, and sorry again!" while I take the kid's place as a visiting prospective student right down to parting my hair down the middle so I more closely resemble the photo that Mr. and Mrs. Bloch sent in the Wednesday before.

"Call me Binny," I say.

"Binny? Who's—"

"Ezra!" an adult calls out from the front of the room. Black suit. Striped prayer shawl draped over his shoulders. His own set of tefillin latched to his arm and head. "Technically, you turned thirteen today, so you're already officially a bar mitzvah. Mazel tov!" He holds out a hand toward a small wooden podium set up near the front of the room. "Why don't you lead us at the amud?"

Ezra rolls his eyes. "No, thanks, Rebbe." A line he's used before.

But we're not here to repeat our old loops. We've got cycles to break, patterns to, um, unpattern. I jab an elbow into Ezra's side.

He looks at me. I look at him. He shakes his head. I nod. And eventually he rolls his eyes again, stands, and steps forward.

"Fine."

The rabbi does a double take. He might not remember all of Ezra's old loops, but you can tell he can predict the future a little anyway, see where Ezra was going because of where he's been. But that was before ol' Finn came to town. And now Ezra's on a new path. I raise a palm at the kid standing next to me, the multiversal transtemporal signal for "high five!" The kid obliges and gives me the tefillin'd victory five I so deserve.

"Excellent!" the rabbi says. "Wow! That's fantastic. Okay, talmidim, birchos hashachar starting on page eight. Ezra, when you're ready, take it away."

And slowly, haltingly, head turned back at me in annoyance a few times . . . Ezra does, in fact, take it away. I'm not sure it's the most rousing Friday morning Jewish day school prayer sesh. High Five Kid next to me falls asleep halfway through. But change is change.

"What's next?" I ask Ezra, rubbing my palms together. The service is over and YBT does breakfast in school:

single-serving cereal boxes and those little milk cartons that look like tiny cardboard houses.

"Next?" Ezra says back. "Does there have to be a—"

Before he can finish, three more kids approach our table.

"Ezra!"

"Big weekend!"

"Look who davened for the amud. Our little boy is all grow'd up!" That last kid—the biggest of the group—wipes a fake tear and pinches Ezra's cheeks. Then they all start singing "Siman tov, u'mazel tov," wrapping Ezra in a hug that would give even my very huggy parents a run for their money.

I scoot closer to Ezra, make myself known. I'm not here for hugs. They all sit.

"Who's the new guy?" one of the kids asks, guzzling a thing of cereal straight out of the packet.

"This is Fi—"

I kick him under the table.

He raises an eyebrow so high, I'm worried it might blast off his face. His way of silently saying: *It doesn't matter what they call you.*

I fast-blink. My way of silently saying: *But I worked so hard on this backstory!*

He groans. "Ugh. Guys, this is Binny. Binny, the guys.

Shai, Dovi, and Menachem Mendel."

I shake all their hands across the table. "An absolute pleasure to meet you Shai, Dovi, and Menachem Mendel."

Ezra groans again, and I take in the group. Shai's got a little mustache going and should probably start shaving soon. Dovi's got a birthmark below his left eye that looks a lot like Texas upside down. And Menachem Mendel is mega-sized, at least two heads taller than the rest.

"I'm visiting for the day!" I continue. "Considering switching from my school to this fine institution. Ezra and I are old family friends. He's very graciously showing me the ropes around here."

Menachem Mendel laughs so hard that milk comes out his nose. "*Ezra?* He barely knows the ropes himself." Menachem Mendel quickly gets serious, his face turning red. "Sorry, Ez. But I mean, you know, right?"

This is why I'm here. I've staked out YBT enough to know that Ezra's not exactly a top student. But I need all the intel I can get if we're gonna achieve peak loop.

"Tell me more," I say.

"Yes," Ezra says, leaning forward, eyebrow now raised at his friends. "Tell us more."

Shai puts an arm around Ezra's shoulders. "We love our friend Ezra here," Shai says. "We'd do anything for him. But school's not his thing. He doesn't like to, you know, *try*."

Ezra sits up again, puts a palm to his chest. "I *try*!" he says.

Menachem Mendel snorts again. "When was the last time you broke a five out of ten on Rabbi Bekenstein's Friday Mishnah quiz?"

"That doesn't mean I don't *try*," Ezra complains. "And none of you are exactly geniuses either."

Shai breathes an exaggerated gasp. "How dare you. I am absolutely a genius. Behold!" He points to a pyramid of six cereal boxes he's built in front of him. "I'd like to see a non-genius do that."

Dovi chuckles, topples the pyramid, and turns back to Ezra. "When was the last time you even *studied* for the Friday quiz?"

Ezra looks around the table at his friends, opens his mouth, closes it again. This is good. This is *very* good. The picture is coming into focus.

"Well," I say to the group, leaning back. "It's a good thing I'm here. We're gonna turn this ship around, aren't we, boys? Get Ezra back in the game."

Shai tilts his head at me. "Aren't you, like, only here for the day?"

I nod. "Best make the most of it, then?"

✳ ✳ ✳

Right. So. School *is* my specialty. Even in a time loop, I can't totally control my parents—they helicopter over me no matter what I do or say. I can't control my classmates—they don't get me; I don't get them. But school? *Grades?* That, I can control. *Here's* the material. *That's* the homework. *There's* the test. 1 + 1 = 2. Voilà.

But this might be harder than I thought.

We head from breakfast to language arts (where Ezra sits in the nosebleed section of the classroom and hasn't so much as cracked open his copy of *Macbeth*). Language arts to something called "Chumash" (where Ezra appears to have lost his copy of the all-Hebrew book they're using). Chumash to math (where it's possible the guy doesn't even know what geometry *is*). Math to lunch (thank the time lords, hard to fail that one). Lunch to life sciences (where somehow Ezra can remember "King Phillip came over for grandma's soup" but has no idea what it stands for). And life sciences to the aforementioned Mishnah class, the study of some kind of old-school Jewish encyclopedia of rules.

Case in point: Did you know that—per Order IV ("Nezikin"), Tractate 1 ("Bava Kamma"), Chapter 4, Mishnah 1—Rabbi Meir and Rabbi Shimon disagree over how much money the owner of an ox should pay if that ox hurts a bunch of other oxes?!

Yeah, me neither. Thrilling stuff. Also, Ezra neither, even though the class meets three times a week. Kid's instinct is to answer the weekly multiple-choice quiz by *circling "C" for every question*. ("As in Chaim," he explains to me, which I think is supposed to be a joke, but makes about as much sense as the Great Ox Debate of 189 AD.) So, during lunch, I insist that Ezra and I review (and review and review) the Mishnah in question. Shai, Dovi, and Menachem Mendel join in too, volunteering their notes and flash cards and Hebrew-English dictionaries.

"Anything for our bar mitzvah boy," Dovi says.

We're minutes from the end of the day. Moment of truth. Can Ezra change or can't he? The Mishnah quiz is given every Loop-Friday and graded toward the end of class.

"Ezra!" Rabbi Bekenstein cheers as he hands back the marked-up quizzes. I lean over his desk, watch him flip the graded quiz right side up. He got 7/10. A solid C. ("As in Chaim"?) Could be better. But could be worse.

"Really delighted at your performance today," Rabbi Bekenstein says. "I can tell you prepared for class, and I'm glad to see it. Let's keep things up on Monday!"

The word always sends a chill down my spine. "Glorious, spectacular Monday," I whisper under my breath.

Shai, Dovi, and Menachem Mendel crowd around Ezra's desk as the bell rings out. They pat him on the back. Fake-punch him on the shoulders. Raise up his arms in triumph.

"Well, well, well."

"Would you look at that!"

"'Really *de-light-ed*.'"

Ezra stays silent and seated as his friends disperse, grab their backpacks, head for the door. We're alone, and I wait for him to say something. And wait. And wait.

"Well?" I blurt out. "I know we've got our work cut out for us, but the universe will reward the effort, trust me."

More silence. "Come on. Say something. Please?"

Another few seconds go by and then—

"No offense," Ezra finally says. "You sure you know what you're doing? It's one random seventh-grade Mishnah quiz. Why would the universe care about one random seventh-grade Mishnah quiz?"

I stand up, pace the room with my hands open wide. "It's all connected. Time, space." I pick up a single Mike and Ike someone had dropped on the floor. "From the smallest atom." I spin the globe perched on Rabbi Bekenstein's desk. "To entire worlds."

He squints at me, not entirely convinced. "That was a nice speech. But do you, like, actually know anything?

Or are you making this up as you go along?"

A bubble of nervousness flutters up from my stomach to my chest. I push it down.

"Only one way to find out," I say, popping the Mike and Ike in my mouth—cherry, good sign—then I slap Ezra's desk and pump my fist in the air. "Let's run it again."

✦ 5 ✦

EZRA

Finn is kind of *a lot*. Which is why it's (almost) a relief when the school day ends each "Loop-Friday," or whatever he calls it. Shabbos dinner with my family isn't any better the millionth time around, but at least Finn isn't here to—

"Hiya!" Finn says, clapping me on the shoulder.

I turn around, and there he is, sitting in the row behind me. Suit and tie. Black yarmulke. Siddur open in his lap to the right page.

It's crowded in shul tonight. It's always crowded in shul every tonight. We haven't even hit Lecha Dodi and the place is standing room only. My dad says our synagogue, Kehillat Beis Meir, wasn't always like this, but I don't remember it any other way. Thirty rows of built-in seats that are full to bursting. Extra folding chairs set up in the aisle. At least two dozen people in the way back, swaying on their heels.

And somehow, Finn's managed to snag the perfect seat, right behind me.

"Lemme guess," I try, imagining all the ways he might have scammed some poor guy out of his chair. "Even though most everyone here doesn't carry a phone on Shabbos, you got ahold of the community directory and figured out the exceptions, like . . . a doctor or . . . an EMT. Then you placed an emergency call to the right dispatcher, which led to whoever was sitting in that exact chair. He bolted out to save someone's life or whatever, but it was you all along. And you've actually been here before, and I never noticed."

"Shhh," my dad grunts, tapping his siddur. He's in our usual row, sitting between me on his left and Eitan on his right. We aren't supposed to talk in shul. And my dad is kind of the unofficial "No Talking" police, this weekend more than most.

"Nah," Finn says. "It's my first time here. I kinda just walked in. But I like the way you're starting to think. WWFD."

"WWFD?"

"What would Finn do? Great motto to live by."

My dad taps his siddur again, harder this time. "Shhh!"

I gesture my head toward the back of the room and sidle out of the row. Finn follows.

"I don't understand," I say, once we're out of earshot of my dad. "I thought we were still working on the school day. I saw you a few hours ago."

When *his* parents arrived exactly on time to pick him up from a school he doesn't even go to. Meanwhile, I always have to wait like an hour for my mom, who shows up late to Friday carpool, no good excuse, Esty screaming from the back seat the whole ride home.

"True true," Finn says. "But I got to thinking—it's been five loops and we're seriously nailing it at school. I mean, yeah, it's not perfect yet. We haven't made a dent in that math lesson. And I still think there's real opportunity in Chumash class to both improve your grade *and* help Shai work up the courage to ask Mrs. Michelson for that extra credit assignment he's been itching for. And then, of course, we've gotta do something about the ol' attitude." He presses his index fingers into his cheeks, pulling his face into a smile. "Turn that frown upside down and all that. But I think we're close. Time to start working on Phase Two."

"Phase Two?"

"Friday night dinner! All that tension at home! No way we break out of here until you're one big happy family."

I must have growled at him out loud, because that smile instantly disappears.

"Are you . . . are you mad at me?" he asks.

Maybe I am, a little. What does any of this have to do with anything? When I first saw Finn standing there in Ballroom C, I thought he was the solution. Then we met in the lobby of the Bergenville, and he told me about time loops and shimmering rainbow portals and stuff. And I was even more sure: This kid was going to rescue us. I was going to get back to my real life. And now . . .

"I thought it would be easier, is all. I'm just *so* tired of this weekend."

"You and me both, brother. But we have to put in the work. I'm *positive* this plan will do the trick. It has to."

"Okay, fine," I say. "I'll trust you. So what do we do now?"

Finn's smile returns. "You invite your favorite time buddy over for the big dinner, and we take it from there." He looks up at the ceiling—something he does every time he thinks something through. "Problem is, I spent most of my recon loops working the YBT angle. I don't yet know how to talk my way into your house."

"Oh," I start. "That's not—"

"Should we come up with another alias for me?" Finn interrupts. "It'll have to be airtight. 'Finn? Who's Finn?'" He gazes around the shul: at all the men in yarmulkes or black hats, the women with covered hair and long sleeves, the rabbi up front with his salt-and-pepper beard. "Not a dude who goes here, I'll tell you that. I've got to be a person your parents would be willing to let into their lives." He taps someone on the shoulder. "Hey, what's your name?"

"Pinchas."

"Pinchas! Solid." He turns back to me. "I'm Pinchas now too. Where can I get me one of those evil rodeo hats?"

I try again. "Seriously, you don't have to—"

"Or . . . think your emergency call idea has legs? Maybe *I* have some emergency? Someone in my own family is sick or something? Yeah, that could work. And that's why I need to eat with you last minute on Friday night. Shouldn't be anything intense though. Don't need them asking too many questions. How about this? We brainstorm over the next few loops, sketch out some concepts—maybe a mood board—throw it all at the wall and see what sticks."

I wait a few seconds, as Finn inhales oxygen for the first time in a full minute. "Are you done?"

Without waiting for an answer, I lead Finn back up the aisle toward my family's row.

"Abba," I say. He's right where we left him. Shuckling back and forth, head down in concentration, mouth moving in silent prayer. "My friend Finn's coming for dinner too, okay?"

Without looking up, Abba just nods and goes, "Shhh!"

"This is it," I tell Finn as we step through the front door. "Is it everything you've been dreaming of?"

Our house is small: kitchen with only one sink. Cramped living room/dining room, everything from IKEA. Four bedrooms—one for my parents; one for Avital; one for me and Eitan; and another for Esty and Eliana. (These last two are really *one* bedroom that my parents split with a wall down the middle.)

And the house keeps getting smaller: We moved in when I was little, and I didn't know how good I had it. Eliana and Esty weren't born yet. Eitan and I had our own rooms. Soon we crammed two more kids into the same space, all five of us got bigger, and the block started to change.

The Frisches went first. Some new family bought

their house, knocked the whole thing down, and built something twice its size on top. Then the same thing happened to the Hararis, and the Carmelis, and the Bargmanns. The new families are nice. Some of them go to our shul. Sruli Milgrom's even invited me over a couple of times to play Monopoly on Shabbos afternoon. But then I have to walk back across the street, which is kind of like rounding from Boardwalk to Mediterranean Avenue, *without* collecting $200.

"It's a great house!" Finn says, admiring the—what? Crayon on the walls? Bowed bookshelves? Scratched table set for ten people who are going to be crammed up against each other all night?

I'm not sure if Finn's being sincere or sarcastic. I'm also not sure which would make me more annoyed.

My father immediately gets started and calls us to the dining room. Around the table clockwise, it's him and my mom; Avital, Eitan, and Eliana (Esty's already asleep in her crib); me and Finn at the far end of the table; and finally Shai, Dovi, and Menachem Mendel, who followed us home after shul, even though all of them live on the other side of town.

For a second, I let myself think that—with someone new—things might be different this time. But Finn doesn't say a single word as we start in on the usual pre-eating Shabbos dinner routine: Shalom Aleichem and Eishes Chayil (a few minutes of songs). Making kiddush (some grape juice) and hamotzi (some challah). Finn's presence changes nothing, so nothing changes. And the moment we all start eating—

Abba, to Avital: "How was your week?"

Avital, without looking up: "You know how it was."

Abba: "Avital, you need to have more respect."

Imma: "Yosef, please. Can we move along?"

Avital: "And can you give someone else a hard time? Let's all gang up on Eitan for a change."

Eitan: "Hey! Why are you bringing *me* into this?!"

Imma: "Can we please try to make it in peace to the other side of Ezra's bar mitzvah and *then* hash this out?"

It takes a full five minutes of arguing before Avital will apologize enough for our dad to leave her alone—Finn scribbling notes under the table with a tiny golf pencil, until I remind him that writing technically isn't allowed here on Shabbos.

"So what's your *deal*?" Finn asks Avital, once my parents get up to serve the main course. He rests his chin in crisscrossed fingers, leans forward even more than usual.

"My deal?"

"Yeah," Finn continues. "Why are you and your dad always arguing? What are your hopes and dreams? What makes the *real* Avital Rosen tick?"

Avital glares at Finn, looks at me, looks back. "I'm sorry, have we *ever* met?"

Finn spears a whole kreplach and shoves it in his mouth. "Not in this universe anyway!" he jokes.

Dovi scratches his head. "I thought you were old family friends," he says to me. The excuse Finn usually dishes out at school on Fridays.

I sit back, cross my arms, not hating the idea of Finn getting caught up in his lies, throwing dinner off course.

"Dovi, Dovi, Dovi," Finn says at a snail's pace, clearly buying time to try to come up with some explanation. "Perceptive, attentive, Dovi. I'm from . . . the other side of the family. Yeah, that's it. The other side."

Which doesn't make sense either, but Dovi doesn't care, and Avital's back to ignoring us all anyway.

My parents return to the table with a tray of schnitzel and potato kugel. Finn turns to my mom, bats his eyelashes. "How about you, Mrs. Rosen? How are *you* doing? How's life treating you?"

She smiles at him. "Aren't you sweet. I'm fine." She clasps my hand for a moment. "Everything is wonderful, baruch Hashem. We have each other. I can't complain."

"Good to hear," Finn says.

Eliana pulls at Finn's sleeve. "You didn't ask how I am!"

"You'll be better if you reinforce the structural integrity of that third floor before Esty wakes up and Godzilla's the thing," he says.

Eliana's eyes go wide with understanding, and she bolts out of the room, taking the creaky steps two at a time.

Suddenly—right on cue—it starts to rain.

"I didn't know we were expecting a storm," I mouth along with my mom, who gets up to refill the water pitcher and grab a fresh seltzer from the fridge.

"Can I go now?" Avital asks; I whisper the same words under my breath.

Abba snaps his head around. "No you cannot *go*. We haven't even sung zemiros yet." Mid-meal songs. My dad likes to sing at least three on Friday night. "It's Ezra's bar mitzvah Shabbos. You're going to skip zemiros on Ezra's bar mitzvah Shabbos?"

Avital groans at me. "Ezra, may I pretty please skip zemiros on your bar mitzvah Shabbos?"

I have given all sorts of answers to this question:

Smiling, nodding. "No problem."

Chucking my cup of water at the wall, swiping my plate to the floor, flipping the table over. "How dare you?!"

Pointing at myself, confused. "Ezra? Who's Ezra?"

But nothing ever changes. And I've stopped responding. This time, I hold up a hand where Finn can see it, show him five fingers, four, three, two, one.

Avital: "I'm leaving."

Abba: "No, you are not."

Imma: "Let her go, Yosef."

My dad turns to my mom, wordlessly begging her to take his side. Avital huffs out of the house. A minute passes. Just chewing and fork clanking and silence too awkward to cut with anything but a challah knife.

Imma: "I'm taking a walk too."

Abba: "In the rain? By yourself?"

"I'll find Avital." My mom scans the table. "Anyone want to come with me?"

No one answers. But the moment she heads out the front door, Eitan leaps up from the table.

"Yeah, I'm out too!" he shouts, sprinting to his room.

The rest of us just sit there: my dad, his face still scrunched up from the argument with Avital. My friends, trying to pretend like they're having a good time. Finn, grinning from ear to ear.

"Is this fun for you?" I ask.

"I am having the time of my life," he says sincerely.

I watch the Shabbos candles flicker—seven flames, one for each member of our family—the light nearly spent. My father distributes pamphlets around the table.

"Let's bench," he says.

When the concluding prayers are done, it all ends like it always does. We nibble at dessert—washed grapes and half-eaten brownies (Eitan's already inhaled a giant corner in secret)—while Shai, Dovi, and Menachem Mendel make conversation:

"You ready for your parsha?"

"Are you speaking in shul, or on Sunday?"

"Can I have a corner piece too?"

Then they go home. Like always, Abba moves to the couch, opens a book, and immediately falls asleep. Like always, my mom and Avital return from their walk, serious, silent, and both soaking wet.

The only thing new is Finn, all the help *he's* been. He starts pacing the width of the kitchen, back and forth, repeating half phrases he heard around the table tonight.

"Well, that was a complete failure," I say.

He stops in his tracks. "A *failure*? No! That was *amazing*. I love your family. And your friends! Ohmygoodness. Do you even *know*?" He puts his hands on my shoulders, stares me down. "But forget your friends for a second. There's something *here*, Ezra. Something *wrong*. Something to *fix*."

"The only thing *here* is my annoying family in our awful house."

"*Yes*. Exactly right. That's what I'm saying. Avital. Your parents. This whole family. It's a puzzle." Finn takes a deep breath, lifts his chin high. "And we're going to solve it."

⋆ 6 ⋆

FINN

But first, my guy needs a break. We've been pushing nonstop. He's earned it. So I told Ezra to take the loop off, that I'd see him again on the next go.

Besides, I've got business to attend to myself. Ezra's got, you know, friends. They follow him around and help him at school and come to his house—and he doesn't even have to *do* anything. Maybe with a little time-loop elbow grease, I can turn my own ship around.

"Rise and shine, Your Majesty!"

"I'm up, I'm up!" I say, throwing off the covers, bringing myself to sitting.

My mom smiles, rests herself on the edge of my bed,

clears her throat. "The early Finn gets the worm!" she says, which is a new one. Always fun to get fresh dialogue.

"I think," I declare, "that I'm going to school today."

My mom laughs. "I should hope so." She pauses. Runs a hand through her hair. "Unless you want to have a family day. Me and your dad can always call in sick. Start the bar mitzvah festivities a little early?"

"Yeah, I know, Mom. Not now. Maybe next-this-Friday, okay? Today I'm on a mission."

"Oh yeah? What's that?"

And I know she'll never remember this conversation. But still. There's something mortally embarrassing about admitting out loud *to your mom* that you don't have any friends, even if this particular mom will evaporate in a few days, replaced by another model off the assembly timeline.

So instead of answering her question directly, I come at it from the side. Try for something general. "Do you think every problem can be fixed?"

She stands, eyes me up and down. "What are you getting at, exactly?" And before I can rephrase, she says, "You know what, maybe your father should be here for this. Leo!"

Immediately, Dad springs into action. Downstairs in the kitchen, a bowl and spoon clang-crash into the sink. He takes the stairs so fast that he's up here in like four seconds flat, panting, hands on his knees.

"What . . . ?" he starts. "Is everything . . . ?"

"We're all fine," my mom says. "Although *you* might be out of shape."

He squints at her, smiles. "Fair. So . . . what's up?"

Catching his breath, Dad swivels my desk chair and sits the wrong way around, legs flanking the back like an uncool teacher trying to talk sense. My mom stands behind him, gently rests a hand on his shoulder. Classic my parents, calling a family meeting at the crack of dawn because I asked a single question.

"Really," I say. "It's nothing. I was just—"

"Finn was asking if every problem can be solved."

My dad looks up at her, tilts his head. She smirks, crinkles her nose. I regret everything. Here it comes:

Why don't we all skip school and work today, hash it out over pancakes?

It's us against the world, kiddo.

We adore you, no matter what.

Because of course they think every problem can be solved, with, like, the love of a parent. I resist the urge to contort my face into the barf-guy emoji.

But they don't say any of that. I get more new dialogue instead.

My dad stands, puts his arm around my mom. "Funny. We were just having this exact conversation. It will come as no surprise to anyone that I am an eternal optimist. There's nothing we can't fix, right? Your mom thinks, well—"

"I think that sometimes it's best to accept things for what they are. Some problems don't have a solution."

Not exactly the rah-rah cheerleading I usually get from these two. But I appreciate the honesty. I'm in a new loop here. Nice to know they can still surprise me.

"Okay," I say to my mom. "Some problems don't have a solution. I get that. But how do you know if your problem is one of them?"

"You don't," my mom says. "But we try anyway. Hope for the best. Manage expectations. Make the kindest, smartest choices we can. That way, whether you change your fate or not, at least you gave it a good try." She pauses. Looks at my dad again. Looks back at me. "Do you want to tell us what problem you're trying to sort out, sweetie?"

My dad gasps. "Oh! Or let's all skip school and

work today, hash it out over pancakes!"

And . . . we're back.

"No, thanks," I say, getting up, heading toward the bathroom. "I'm pancaked out."

Everyone files into classroom seven. Lila Waters. Ed Zewail. The Salpeter twins. Kailee Rodriguez. Basically my whole class. Even got three out of the four Ethans. All here to partake in a semi-decent party, if I do say so myself. We've got cone hats. We've got kazoos. Plus as many doughnuts as I could carry from the coffee shop down the block.

Obviously, with a few more loops, I can take things up a notch. Something real classy. Hot breakfast buffet, maybe—waffles, little potatoes, scrambled eggs. Bah! Omelet station! Maybe the Bergenville can cater! And we'll need entertainment too. A photo booth? Karaoke? I wonder if there are any close-up magicians in town.

Still, this is a good start. I let them enjoy for a few minutes, really soak it in. But I know from past-future experience that Assistant Principal Esposito will lock up in here after the next bell. So I call this thing to order, open my arms wide.

"Hello, friends!"

They all turn around, doughnuts in hand.

Ed checks behind him to see if there's anyone else here. "Are you talking to us?" he asks.

"Who else would I be talking to?"

No one responds.

"Well, I wanted to, um, thank you for coming to this pre–bar mitzvah party."

One of the Ethans turns to another. "That's what this is?" he mutters. "The sign on the door says 'free food for seventh graders.'"

I ignore them. "I wanted to express my appreciation to you, my dear classmates, and also, you know, see who might be coming to my actual party this Sunday." Silence. "Don't be shy now."

More silence, more craned necks to the nonexistent kids on the other side of the table.

"Lila?" I try. She's never come to the party, not even one loop.

Lila eyes a spot on the floor. "It's a busy weekend."

"Busy with what?"

"You know, weekend stuff."

"Oh, sure. Can't miss your important *stuff*. *Stuff* only comes around once in a lifetime. What about you, Ed?" Also a regular no-show.

Ed closes one eye, stares at me, then switches, like he's taking an eye exam and can't quite make out the bottom row. "What *about* me? This is the first time you've talked to me all year. Why would I go to your bar mitzvah?"

"That's not true!" I complain, trying to remember life pre-loop. "We talk."

"It doesn't count if it's only 'What do you think will be on the test?' Or 'Can I use your pencil sharpener?' Or 'Did anyone *else* get an A+?' That's not talking."

Grumbles of agreement bounce around the room. A flash of anger rises in my throat. I consider grabbing everyone's doughnuts, chucking them in the garbage.

"Kailee?" I say. "What about you? You're coming on Sunday, right? I know you're coming. I've seen you there!"

She tilts her head. "Seen me there?"

Cover, Finn. Cover.

"I mean, like, um, in my dreams?"

Nope. That was *not* better than the truth.

One of the Ethans laughs. Lila gasps. But Kailee—wonderful, kind, always-comes-to-my-bar-mitzvah Kailee—keeps it together.

"Okay. Well, yeah. I'm coming on Sunday." Then she looks around, even though no one said anything, and defends herself by adding: "My parents are making me."

Et tu, Kailee?

"But why? Why don't any of you want to come?"

Another Ethan steps forward. "Do you even know my name?"

I jut out my chin. "Of course! Ethan!"

"And my *last* name?" I freeze. Something with a "B," right? Or is it a "T"? Ethan pops the rest of a jelly doughnut in his mouth, licks his fingers, grabs another, takes a bite. "I'll wait."

"Okay. I don't know."

"We've been in class together since first grade," Ethan points out.

"Right."

"We took the school bus together for *years*."

"Sure."

"We were paired up to discuss the history reading *two days ago*."

Not exactly the full picture. But that part's not really Ethan's fault. "True. But come on, that can't be *it*. Just because I, you know, care a lot about school and am not great with names. That can't be the only reason none of you want to come on Sunday, right?"

They all look at each other, holding back. "It's cool. I promise. Permission to speak freely."

Shane Salpeter steps forward and goes, "Well, you're kind of . . . a know-it-all?"

Nods of agreement.

Ed goes, "Yes!"

Ethan [LAST NAME] chimes in: "I was going to say 'smart alex.'"

"I think you mean, 'smart aleck,'" I correct. They all stare at me. "Not helping my case. I see that now."

Shane points at Ethan in agreement. "He's right, though. Smart alex, smart aleck, whatever."

Lila: "You're always bossing people around, telling us what to do, even when no one's asked. You say you care a lot about school, but it feels like that's the *only thing* you care about."

Ed: "You don't, you know, seem to like *us* very much."

"Okay!" I say, a knot in my chest. "Message received. I get it. But look!" I gesture at the table. "A peace offering. Doughnuts! You can't still be mad at me after I brought in doughnuts."

For what seems like the millionth time, the room goes silent. No one says a word, and each passing second feels like forever. Then the bell rings and kids shuffle to the exit, still mostly silent, except Ethan [LAST NAME], who takes a whole dozen doughnuts to go, and says, "It's Bonsor, by the way."

I knew it had a "B."

The room clears. In seconds, only Kailee is left,

standing in the doorway. "What did you think was going to happen here?" she asks. "That you could snap your fingers, bring us breakfast, and we'd completely forget years of you mostly ignoring us?"

Well, when she puts it like that. "What if I'd hired someone to do close-up magic?" I ask, mostly a joke.

She laughs. "That might have been worse."

"I guess I was hoping . . . ," I say, "that this was a problem with a solution. I had to try."

She nods. "I get that. But this is only *one day*. What about yesterday?"

"Yes-ter-day?" I echo.

"Yeah, you know, the day before today."

"The day before today," I repeat, snorting. "Wild."

She looks at me weird but pushes on anyway. "I only mean that we can't forget yesterday and the day before that and the day before that all because you say you've changed *today*. Things take time."

Something I have way, way too much of and apparently not nearly enough. Kailee smiles.

"It's nice you want to try. And *I'll* still be there on Sunday, even if my parents *don't* make me."

She sticks out her tongue. I laugh.

"And then, I don't know, forget this whole bribing us

thing. Sit with us at lunch next week or something. Me, Lila, Ed. Hang out. Just . . . be cool. You know, start fresh on Monday."

I breathe in. Breathe out. Biggest sigh of my life. "Yeah. Will do."

If I can ever get there.

7

EZRA

"I didn't know we were expecting a storm."

Here we go again.

Finn's right. I did need a break. But going through this dinner alone isn't exactly my idea of a good time. It all goes the same. It always goes the same. I picture Finn somewhere out there, doing whatever Finn does when he's not haunting my life—hammocking on a beach, probably. His dad holding a coconut to his mouth so Finn can drink through the straw without lifting his hands. His mom fanning him with a giant palm branch. Both showering him with all that unconditional love he seems to hate. Poor baby.

This dinner is like the opposite of that.

Avital: "I'm leaving."

Abba: "No, you are not."

Imma: "Let her go, Yosef."

I considered skipping out on the whole thing this time. Not showing up on Friday night. Refusing to do my Torah reading on Saturday. Being somewhere else—anywhere else—on Sunday. They'd all reset anyway. But that first Shabbos day I walked to meet Finn at the Bergenville did not go well. The day ended with me coming home to police officers gathered around our living room, all my friends waiting for me, my mother in tears, my dad quieter than ever, like he'd shushed *himself* into total silence. The man did not speak another word to me all weekend. No one did. Except Avital, who barged into my room late Saturday night, shouting—"You are *not* the only one in this family"—and slamming the door behind her.

More confirmation that—even when they think I'm literally *lost*—the weekend is still about *them*. I don't know how Finn does it. Always finding ways to be with me in my loop. He says he has perfect excuses for every occasion. It's probably true. That, and perfect parents.

"I'm taking a walk too," my mom says, after Avital breaks away from the table. At least we're almost done here. Then I can eat a brownie. Go to bed.

"In the rain?" my dad asks. "By yourself?"

"I'll find Avital." My mom glances around. "Anyone want to come with me?"

As usual, no one does. She leaves alone. Eitan jets to his room. My dad grabs benchers. And then—

"You know what, hold on," I say, trying something different, turning to Shai, Dovi, and Menachem Mendel. "I'm going to go too, okay?"

"For sure."

"No problem!"

"Absolutely."

This isn't WWFD. Or, not exactly. There's no way I'm ever getting inside that kid's head. *What would Finn do?*—no, thank you. Maybe: *What would Ezra do?* No one's looking out for me but me. Time to start making a few choices of my own.

"Thanks," I say, and follow my mom out the door.

From the dry safety of our front stoop, I scan in all directions for my mom and Avital. It might not be possible to catch up with them. It's been a minute—and all I know is that they eventually return together, all wet. They could be anywhere. Across the street at the Milgroms' house. Down to either end of the block. Maybe in the playground or at shul or—

"Ezra!" my mom says.

—or not.

"I was about to go search for Avital," she tells me.

Imma is standing a few feet to my left, also completely dry. She's underneath the covered overhang that stretches from above our front door to the garage. Her hand is up, gripping the metal handle to manually slide the garage door down.

She lets go when she sees me, beckoning me inside the garage, away from the rain. I haven't been in here in a week, which means I haven't been in here in many, many weeks. Somebody's been organizing, but also doing the opposite. There are bins of old clothes stacked in a corner. Piles of books underneath handwritten signs: "Keep," "Donate." And we must have missed a recycling day or two, because cardboard boxes are spilling out of the yellow bin.

"Mess in here, isn't it?" my mom says, looking embarrassed.

"Yeah," I agree.

She drags two bins across the concrete floor, sits down on one. "I'm glad you're here," she says, patting the bin next to her.

I sit. "You are?"

She turns to me. "Of course. *Always*."

I'm not sure I believe it. But I want to.

She keeps staring at me, like she's searching for something in my face, like there's more she wants to say. I fill the silence in my mind with what I imagine Finn's parents are saying to him right now: *We love you. We're so proud of you. You're the center of the world.* Blah blah blah. But Imma doesn't actually say anything. And I don't push. Instead, we face forward again, watch the rain sheet down on the other side of the garage door, listen to its pitter on the roof, the cars, the grass.

Then Avital lurches up the driveway, sopping wet. She doesn't see us at first, turning toward the front door. But something catches in her vision, and she stops, spins, squints into the garage.

Avital looks at me. Looks at Imma. Looks at all the boxes. "Mess in here, isn't it?!" she shouts, using the same words and tone as our mom, just ten times as loud to be heard through the storm.

Now I'm no stranger to hearing people say the same things over and over. But the repeat line *here* makes me giggle. Then my mom laughs. Then all three of us are laughing, doubled over for no reason at all. I spot a dry, clean, folded beach towel on the floor, left over from some drive down to the shore. I toss it to Avital without thinking.

"Wanna dry off?"

But the rain is falling in buckets and the dry towel is *immediately* drenched. It thunks to the ground like a brick.

"Gee, thanks!" Avital says sarcastically, picking up the wet towel, unfurling it like a picnic blanket she's about to lay in the grass. She pretends to dry off, patting her hair, rubbing her arms. That gets us all cracking up even more.

"Okay," our mom says. "Let's get you inside before you catch cold."

"You know that's not a thing, right, Imma?"

"I know I'm your mother and have wiped approximately ten million boogers in these eighteen years of your life, so I win this conversation, whether it's *a thing* or not."

Avital takes a little bow in the rain—"Strong argument"—and comes inside. She dries off (with a new towel) while we each take turns saying, "Mess in here, isn't it?" in different accents. Once she's dry, we reenter the house through the mudroom door. And this time, for the first time, my mom walks back in happy, loud, not a drop of rain on her.

8

FINN

"There is no way *this* is in any of your time-loop movies," Ezra says the next go-round.

"True," I admit. "But we've got to be willing to innovate here."

"And you're sure you don't want to take another loop off?" Ezra asks. "I do my own thing a little longer, you do yours?"

Know-it-all.

Smart aleck.

"Yeah, I'm sure. Time to get back to work."

First, I'm thinking a little background is in order. At my family's temple—Rodeph Ahava—everyone sits together. At Ezra's, men and women sit apart. At ours, a lot of the service is in English, said or sung out loud together. At Ezra's, it's all in Hebrew, a lot of it said quietly, by each person individually. At ours, for my bar mitzvah, I read only the haftorah. But Ezra's show is something else entirely—a whole Torah reading, haftorah, all the frills.

And if you want to know what the Torah reading and haftorah *are*, well, let's start with a different question: What is Hebrew?

Well, it's a lot of things. And one of those things is a written language that doesn't have vowel letters. If that sentence makes no sense, don't worry. I didn't get it at first either. But think about it. The English vowels are: A, E, I, O, U (and maybe Y sometimes, right?). The vowels are *in* the alphabet. But let's say you *removed* them and saw this word:

"CLCK."

Is it a ticking *clock*? Is it the *click* of a button? The *cluck* of a chicken? No clue. You need context, or at least vowels. And that's Hebrew: A written language that *doesn't* include vowels as letters. Instead, the vowels (called "nekudot") are sometimes (and only sometimes) written as tiny symbols above and below the letters. A little dot here, a little line there.

The heart of the Shabbat service in both mine and

Ezra's synagogues starts with someone reading from the Torah and ends with someone reading the haftorah. The haftorah is short and read from a book that includes nekudot. The Torah reading is *loooong* and read from a giant scroll that doesn't have nekudot. You need to memorize *all of them* in advance of the bar mitzvah, plus singsongy musical notes for *each word*.

TLDR: Haftorah reading = kind of hard. Torah reading = super hard.

And they make thirteen-year-old kids do this stuff.
For their birthdays.

I think Ezra did okay, despite some random guy telling him—"Nu, a little flat"—after the reading was done. Truth is, I was too distracted to pay close attention, take in all the clues.

I kept staring at the Torah itself.

I mean, think about it. Giant scroll of ancient words that can only be read with intense practice and great focus. Ink hand-quilled onto parchment, written in this special Torah font that spins out these mysterious little crowns growing out of the Hebrew letters. It's got enormous wooden handles, like hilts on medieval swords. They even use this fancy silver pointer thingy to follow along. The end is fashioned into—get this!—a teeny little hand. It is not a magic wand. But it is the closest thing to a magic wand that I have ever seen in real life.

Does the Torah scroll have the power to fix the flow of time? *Probably not.* But is it possible . . . ? Frankly, it would be time-loop negligence not to consider all the options.

Ezra's still dragging his feet. "Don't you have your own bar mitzvah to be at?" he asks. "Where are your parents?"

"Don't worry about them," I answer. "They'll be fine."

And they will. I'm working on the right lines to get them to come *here* on Saturday. Maybe convince them that my new buddy Ezra needs my support. Maybe get Ezra's synagogue to swap me in for the haftorah. Something. I'll get there. For now, my parents are . . . wherever they are. I just kinda left. Reset is in a day anyway. And I am not super devastated to be apart from them. I'd like a break from being constantly smacked in the face by the reality that the only people in my life who like me are my *mom* and *dad*.

"Stop looking for excuses," I say. "Let's do this thing."

"All right," Ezra breathes. "What do you want to do?"

The service is long over. Ezra's family is in the synagogue social hall, where the congregation is throwing a lunch buffet in honor of Ezra's bar mitzvah. Ezra and I are still in the sanctuary, standing at the front, staring at what my temple calls the "ark" and what Ezra calls the "aron"—a.k.a. the Torah scroll closet.

Portal gate, anyone?

The coast being clear, I drag open the outer velvet curtain and pull back on the wooden doors protecting the scrolls. Above our heads is a flickering electric light, made to look like a small fire. Rodeph Ahava has one too. Ezra tells me it's called a "Ner Tamid," which he translates as "Everlasting Fire." And if that's not a perfect time-travelly Easter egg, what is?

There are two Torahs inside this aron, latched behind a metal chain that's hooked crossways to prevent the heavy scrolls from pitching forward.

"Should we take them out?" I ask. "I hold one, you hold one?"

Ezra looks at me like I have two heads, so I back off. "How about we each touch one? Can we at least put our hands on them?"

He is *not* enjoying this experiment, which I can tell, because I'm such a careful student of the human condition, and also because he says, "I am *not* enjoying this experiment." He places a palm against the rightmost scroll anyway. And I do the same with the Torah on the left.

"Now what?" he asks.

I hold out my other hand.

"You're kidding," Ezra says. "Please no."

I don't respond, don't move. He grunts but goes along with it. And now we're just two kids, holding hands, touching the epic scrolls. This *has* to be something, right?

"Okay, okay," I say when nothing happens. "We should probably say something."

"How about, 'This is silly. Let's eat,'" Ezra suggests.

"Not productive. We've got to break the spell, right? Maybe we need a spell of our own. How about something like . . ." I close my eyes, concentrate. "'Torah, Torah, hear our rhyme. Torah, Torah, bring back time!'"

I open one eye, then the other, replaying the line in my head. "Right, so that was a garbage spell. But no bad ideas in brainstorming! Besides, I don't hear you coming up with any workable suggestions."

He takes a moment to think. "What about, 'I wish the time loop would end.'"

I consider it. "Simple. To the point. I like it! We should probably say it three times, to be safe." He doesn't reply. I assume he's onboard. "On the count of three, okay?"

"If you say so."

"I do. Okay. Great. And really, this *probably* won't work. Let's not set our expectations too high, okay?"

"I'll try," he says flatly.

"Great," I say again. "Okay, one, two, three—"

"I wish the time loop would end," we say at the same time. "I wish the time loop would end. I wish the time loop would end."

We unclasp our hands, let go of the Torah scrolls, blink at each other.

A new thought occurs to me. "We're still in our own bodies, right?"

Now Ezra glares at me like I have *three* heads. "Why wouldn't we be in our own bodies?!"

"No reason. Just making sure." I rake my hair, pull my earlobes, rub my chin. "I'm definitely still me."

"And we're definitely still stuck in this time loop," Ezra points out.

Could be. No crackle of lightning or chorus of voices or any of the stuff you'd assume would happen if we managed to break the loop. Of course, there's only one way to know for sure. "Let's see what happens at the end."

But what happens is the clock strikes 1:36 p.m. on Loop-Sunday and we go back to the beginning. I know what you're thinking: What if we change the chant to "I *hope* the time loop would end." Great suggestion. Good hustle. But nope. And adding a "please" to the whole thing doesn't do the trick either.

"What if we switch sides this time," I suggest, a few more loops in. "You take the Torah on the left. I touch the one on the right. And maybe we don't hold hands. Maybe we—"

"No," Ezra says. "Nope. I'm done. You enjoy. I'm not doing this anymore."

"What do you mean, *this*?"

He holds out his arms. "This, I'm not doing any of this. The magic spell, for one thing. There's an unlimited combination of words we could say. You get that, right? It's pointless to keep trying." He takes a deep breath, pauses, and adds: "And now that I think about it, the perfect loops are the same."

"How are they the same? What are you talking about? We're getting close!"

"Close to *what*? I'm improving in school. Fine. Friday night is *a bit* better, I guess, now that I know to follow my mom out for her walk. And I think my leining"—what he calls reading from the Torah—"is about as good as it's going to get."

"I don't see the problem then. You're doing exactly what you need to do."

"But where does it *end*? What even *is* a perfect loop?

Perfect to who? *Me?* My parents? Mr. Bendish? You've seen it yourself, it doesn't matter how good I am at leining. Whether or not Eliana barfs on my shoes. Whether or not I make a mistake. Whether or not you bring him that package of Stella D'Oros before davening—"

"I really thought it was a blood sugar thing," I interrupt.

"It's not," Ezra continues. "It's not *anything*. He can't be pleased. Some things never change. No matter what, he still tugs at his suspenders and says—"

"'Nu, a little flat,'" I finish for him. "I know. I've been thinking about that. It's possible Mr. Bendish is a kind of . . . singularity. A static figure in time, who behaves the same no matter how things change from one loop to the next. We need to keep at it. Cracking him might be the answer we're looking for. I'm half convinced he's the key."

"You're half convinced *everything* is the key," Ezra says. "And making *everything* perfect is impossible. It would take forever."

I truly don't get Ezra's problem. "We *have* forever!"

"And I don't want to spend it like this," Ezra declares. "Have *you* actually run a perfect loop? Are you sure? Is everything *really* perfect out there in Finn-Land?"

Know-it-all.

Smart aleck.

I take a step back, cross my arms, try to clear my head. "How can you even say that?"

He snorts. "That isn't an answer. Or is it?"

I don't believe this. Ezra is clearly having a bad day. He can't possibly think he knows better than I do about the way out. I make a mental note to schedule a real vacation loop. Maybe we can get ourselves to Disney on Friday with enough time to enjoy the parks before things reset. For now, I decide to back off.

"If you've got any ideas," I say. "I'm happy to try them."

He walks down the main synagogue aisle and plops into a random seat. "I've got nothing."

I sit down next to him.

"Maybe we need a little help," he says.

"From who?" I ask. "I've tried telling my parents. They never believe me. I know yours don't either."

"I don't mean our families. We need, I don't know, someone on the outside. A fresh perspective. Someone who . . ."

Ezra trails off. I urge him on. "Someone who what?"

"I was going to say: Someone who gives advice for a living."

I raise an eyebrow. "Do we know anyone like that?"

He stands up, eyes wandering to the special chair

at the front of the room, the one reserved for the rabbi. "He's here right now."

"Rabbi Neumann?" I say. "He can't help us."

"How do you know?" Ezra asks, making his way down the aisle. I follow, as Ezra breaks into a sprint and bursts through the doors at the back of the sanctuary.

"WWED! *What would Ezra do?*" he shouts behind him. "No bad ideas in brainstorming!"

I've created a monster.

"It's not going to work," I mumble as we cross the atrium into the social hall. Telling people never works.

Lunch is still going strong. Avital is whispering to her mom in one corner of the room. In the other, Eliana and Esty are flipping through a torn-up picture book. Ezra's dad is smiling and laughing in a small crowd of congregants, but you can tell that no one's really having fun. And closer to one of the buffet tables—set up with the same potato kugel and breaded chicken cutlets the Rosens eat on Friday night—the rabbi's got his hands in the air, waving them around as he makes some point to Mr. Bendish.

"When in reality, Rashi was simply unaware that his conception of popular seals was an anachronism. He couldn't have appreciated that cylinder— Ezra! I was hoping to see you!" The rabbi turns back to Mr. Bendish for a moment. "To be continued, Dovid."

Mr. Bendish grunts and walks away.

"Now, then," the rabbi continues in our direction. "Mazel tov again, young man. I know you've been practicing for a while. But that was some of the best Torah reading I have ever heard from a bar mitzvah boy. Nearly perfect."

Nearly, I mouth in Ezra's direction.

"And who is this?" the rabbi asks, extending a hand for me to shake.

"Finn," I answer. "Finn Einstein." And because I always know the next question, I add, "No relation."

The rabbi chuckles. "Well, very nice to meet you, Finn. Any friend of Ezra's is welcome in our shul anytime. What can I do for you boys?"

Ezra looks at me. I sigh, but give a *Go ahead* shrug. This'll ruin the current run. But like I said, we have forever. What's one wasted loop between friends?

"Okay," Ezra begins. "Okay. The thing is, Finn and I, we're stuck in a . . ." He bites the insides of his cheeks, tries again. "Forget me and Finn for a second. We have a general question for you. Do you maybe know anything about . . . time travel?"

Here comes the laughter and the disbelief and the *Maybe you should lie down.*

"Time travel," the rabbi repeats, scratching at his beard.

"Yeah. Anything at all. Finn and I really need to know *anything* you might be able to tell us about time travel."

At this point, *I* can't help but laugh. But before I can say *I told you so*, the rabbi looks up at the small skylight in the ceiling. And when he dips his head down again, his face is all seriousness. He breathes out heavy through his nose. Removes his reading glasses. Nods like he knows *exactly* what we mean.

"Come with me if you want to learn."

✱ 9 ✱

EZRA

The rabbi leads us to his office, back into the main sanctuary and through a small door near the aron. The room looks exactly as it did last Sunday. The Sunday *before* the loop, I mean. I took bar mitzvah lessons here with the previous rabbi of our shul, Rabbi Alter, before he retired. Technically, Rabbi Neumann's only been in charge a few days. He replaced Rabbi Alter on Wednesday. With all the time looping, I'd forgotten that he was "new" to the community. Feels like I've known him forever.

Wonder why.

"Welcome, welcome," he says, clearing two chairs of unopened boxes.

Same as Rabbi Alter before him, Rabbi Neumann's space is more library than office—wall-to-wall books in 360 degrees, surrounding a simple desk. The desk is a mess: piles of books and papers cover every inch of its surface. There are more boxes on the floor, waiting to be unpacked. He's still moving in. But the shelves are already neat and organized. Small metal plaques list the contents of each section in Hebrew: "Chumash" "Tanach" "Mussar" "Halacha" "Talmud."

"In truth," Rabbi Neumann tells us, "every book in here can transport you in time." He points to a thin English paperback. "This will take you back a year." He taps at another volume, leather bound, Hebrew lettering on the spine. "This will take you back a hundred. And this"—he tilts a thick book backward by the binding, before pushing it back into place—"will move you a thousand."

He glances back at us, a gleam in his eye. "But I take it you boys are hunting for something . . . even older."

"Gotta admit," Finn whispers to me. "Strong start."

And it *is* a strong start. Hope rises in my chest. If I'm being honest, I insisted we try Rabbi Neumann mostly to prove Finn wrong, show him that two could play at this time-loop game. But then, of course the rabbi could help! Last year, Rabbi Alter organized a fundraiser after a hurricane damaged a shul in South Jersey. His family hosted Shai and his mom for Shabbos lunch like a dozen times after his dad moved out. He personally called around town to make a minyan for Dovi's great-aunt's funeral when not enough people showed up. Rabbis *help*. That's what they're *for*.

Rabbi Neumann steps toward the Talmud section and begins dragging a finger across the collection. Twenty-one enormous volumes, golden Hebrew lettering on the spines.

"Let's see. Horayot. Zevachim. Aha! Menachot." He pulls the giant book off the shelf, gently places it atop the pile on his desk, and opens the thick cover. "Now, if I remember correctly . . . ," he continues, flipping pages.

"Here it is," he says, tap-tap-tapping the spot.

Finn and I gather round. Rabbi Neumann begins, translating as he reads: "Rav Yehuda said the following, in the name of Rav. When Moshe Rabbeinu—"

"Moses," I explain for Finn.

"—ascended Mount Sinai, he found God himself sitting and tying little crowns to the letters of the Torah."

"I know those crowns!" Finn says, snapping his fingers. "I *knew* they were important."

"Everything is important to someone," the rabbi says. "We must each decide what is important to *us*. But

I digress." He looks back down into the Gemara and continues. "Moshe said to God, 'Why are you doing this? Why are you adding those crowns?' And God said back, 'Because in the future, after many generations, there will be born a man named Rabbi Akiva, son of Yosef—'"

"OMG, *you're* the son of Yosef!" Finn says to me, shaking with excitement. "And your middle name is Akiva! It's a sign!"

I nod at the rabbi to continue.

"'There will be born,'" Rabbi Neumann repeats, "'a man named Rabbi Akiva, son of Yosef. This Akiva will explain the meaning of every thorn and bump on every crown.' Curious, Moshe tells God, 'Show him to me.' And God obliges. He tells Moshe to turn around—and, when he does, Moshe finds himself in the future.'"

"I'm sorry," I say. "Wait. Moshe traveled in time? Like, brought-us-out-of-Egypt Moshe, got-the-Torah Moshe, led-us-through-the-desert Moshe. *He was a time traveler?*"

Rabbi Neumann shrugs. "It would appear so."

Go figure. Maybe I *should* pay more attention in school.

"Is this a true story?" Finn asks. "Like, did it actually happen?"

Rabbi Neumann tilts his head. "Those two questions

aren't really the same question" is all he responds. "But the story gets better. Moshe is sent forward into the future, to Akiva's time, to Akiva's classroom. And what else does a person do in a classroom but learn? Moshe sits at the end of the eighth row of seats and listens as Akiva explains the meaning of the crowns."

Rabbi Neumann doesn't pause. Finn chimes in anyway: "Well?! What happened next?"

The rabbi taps the page of Gemara. "Something extraordinary. Moshe—our greatest teacher—listened as Rabbi Akiva taught his lesson. And Moshe . . . did not understand a word. He became frustrated. His strength was sapped. And then, Akiva's students spoke up. 'Our teacher,' they said, voicing the very question that was inside Moshe's own mind. 'How do you know all this?'"

Finn is practically hyperventilating. And who could blame him. This really does feel like *it*, like Rabbi Neumann is about to reveal the great secret we've been waiting to hear, light the way out, the way forward.

"Amar la'hen," Rabbi Neumann reads in the original Hebrew, "halacha l'Moshe mi'sinai."

"What does that mean?!" Finn begs, tugging at Rabbi Neumann's jacket sleeve. "What did he say?!"

"He said," the rabbi answers, "'I know this, because it is something Moshe learned at Mount Sinai.'"

He pauses reading. Looks up. A mischievous grin on his face.

Finn lets go of the rabbi's arm, more disappointment on his face than Mr. Bendish after my Torah reading. "That's it?" Finn asks, squinting into the mazelike page of Gemara, texts expanding out from the center in ever-smaller script.

Rabbi Neumann scans a few more lines, wincing a little as he reads. Then his grin returns, and he shuts the book. "That's it! What'd I tell you?! Time travel in the Gemara! A loop of a sort, even. Ein chadash tachat hashemesh!"

Nothing new under the sun. But the rabbi doesn't translate this time, and Finn doesn't ask him to. Instead, Finn falls into one of the two chairs opposite the rabbi's desk and drops his head into his hands.

"We need to know about *real* time travel," he says. "Not, like, metaphorical riddle nonsense."

"Hey!" I shout, standing between him and the rabbi, crossing my arms. "How is that any more metaphorical riddle nonsense than the Hedgehog Day movie you keep telling me about?"

Finn pinches the bridge of his nose. "That's not what it's called, and you know it."

"What I *know* is that I finally suggest an idea of

my own and you doubt me from the start. Meanwhile I'm *constantly* going along with your plans that get us nowhere."

"Oh, please. You complain every loop."

"Because nothing you suggest *works*!"

"And you think this detour is any different?"

"I'm *trying*."

"So am I!"

Rabbi Neumann claps his hands together to get our attention. I think I'd forgotten he was there. Finn too. "I am not entirely sure what this argument is about. But I am sorry I couldn't help you. When you mentioned time travel, that story was simply the first thing that came to mind."

I turn away from Finn. "It's okay, Rabbi. Don't worry about it. Of course you wouldn't know anything about actual time travel."

"I do not," the rabbi says, picking up the Gemara, putting it back on the shelf. "You should probably ask the physicists."

A beat goes by. Finn stands. "What . . . physicists?"

The rabbi angles his head. "You know, the physicists. The ones in town for the weekend. I'm sure *you* know about them, Ezra."

Finn's face cycles through shock and curiosity and delight.

"I don't know anything about any physicists," I say.

"Oh," Rabbi Neumann says. "I only thought because of tomorrow. I'm sure it was at least a conversation with your parents when they were planning." He lowers his voice a bit. "But I know that's more your uncle Chaim's department."

What is he talking about?

"Here," the rabbi says, rummaging around on his desk, splitting the sea of books to reveal a familiar newspaper: *The Bergenville Gazette*. It's one of the small township papers that materialize in everyone's driveway, every week, whether you subscribe or not. Hard-hitting news like the latest houses for sale and whether the Bergenville High Leviathans won their latest junior varsity tennis match.

"Events section," the rabbi says, handing me the folded-up paper.

I take the *Gazette* in my hands and fan it wide, flipping to the events spread at the back. I read the headline: "'Annual Shop-Mart bake sale to benefit park re-mulching'?"

Rabbi Neumann shakes his head. "Not that.

Although I am as excited about the re-mulching as anyone. Check halfway down the page."

"Oh, okay. I think I see it. 'Township welcomes annual'"—I glance at Finn—"'annual convention of nation's leading physicists.'"

"Whoa," Finn breathes. "Is that this week's newspaper?"

I read on. "'Event to feature latest discoveries and innovations across the field, from quantum mechanics to AI modeling to space-time curvature. Three-day conference begins, Friday morning at—'"

I loop back to the beginning, read the line twice, just to be sure.

"That's why I thought you might know about this," the rabbi says. "Given the timing and location."

"Given *what* timing?" Finn asks, locking eyes with me. "*What* location? What is going on?"

I take a deep breath. "'Three-day conference begins,'" I read, "'Friday morning, at the Bergenville Hotel and Convention Center.'"

10

FINN

"Okay, now *this* is probably the key," I say.

Ezra nods. "Going to have to agree with you on that one."

This whole time. The answers have been inside our hotel the whole time. How could I have missed it? I was so focused on sorting out why the universe would trap us in a time loop that I forgot, you know, that the universe trapped us in a time loop. And the most obvious solution to this kind of problem isn't perfect loops or magic spells, it's *science*. I've been treating this thing like I'm stuck in a story. But what I'm really stuck in is my life.

"What does it mean?" Ezra asks.

It's Loop-Sunday, almost noon, and somewhere on

the opposite side of the hotel, our parties are in full swing (or, what passes for full swing, at least). An easy time to sneak off, take in our new situation.

"I've been asking myself that question all night," I say. "There's only one possible answer."

Ezra turns toward me, waiting.

We're standing about a dozen feet from the closed doors of the Main Convention Showroom at the Bergenville, a banner above the doors announcing the "37th Annual Mid-Atlantic Conference of Interdisciplinary Quantum Physicists."

"Think about it," I say as we listen to a muffled voice on the other side of the doors. Someone is giving a speech over a microphone, mixed with polite applause. "It's a physics convention, right? They deal with the universe and particles and time. And it happens to be that we're the ones stuck in this loop? No way. They must have had an accident. Some sort of quantum photon acceleration misfire."

Ezra gives me one of his Ezra looks. "Are you just putting random science words together?"

I wave him away. "It must have happened at exactly one thirty-six p.m., that first loop around. Somewhere nearby, something went wrong with one of their dangerous experiments. They flew too close to the sun. And we're the victims." I grab Ezra by the shirt. "Don't you see! This is it! This is what we have to do. Get into that convention. Find the accident and stop it before it has a chance to get us stuck in time." I stare up at the ceiling, working things through. "Of course, we've got to make sure we don't inadvertently cause the very accident we're setting out to prevent. But one thing at a time."

I look back down and wait for another classic Ezra reaction. Some blend of eye-rolling and nitpicking.

Instead, he nods. "I can't believe I'm saying this. But that all makes perfect sense to me."

I'm beaming. We're finally getting somewhere. Inside those doors is the answer to all our problems. "Shall we?" I ask.

"We shall," Ezra says.

We walk forward, each grab one of the doors, and—

"It's locked," I say, pulling hard, then harder.

Ezra yanks on the door too, shimmies the handle. Nothing. Suddenly, that snooty concierge approaches from around a nearby corner.

"This guy again," I mutter to Ezra.

"Can I help you?" Andy Pauli says. "There's no entry during the keynote." He flares his nostrils on every third word, like we smell bad and he wishes we'd take a shower.

"We're trying to get into the conference," I explain. "We're fine."

He smacks his lips. "I see." Then his mouth coils into an exaggerated smile, and he points at a booth to the side of the locked doors. "Good luck," he says, dropping his hands and marching away, one-two, one-two.

"Man, he's annoying," I say.

Ezra and I walk up to the booth.

The table is stacked with brochures and schedules, sign-in sheets and loose pens. It's all behind a folded placard that reads, "CONFERENCE REGISTRATION," staffed by a bored-looking woman who's doodling directly on the plastic tablecloth.

"Hello," I say, stepping forward as confidently as possible. "Two tickets, please!"

The woman chuckles like I made a joke. But I keep my face steady, and she finally understands.

"Oh! You're serious. Sorry, young man." She scans us up and down. "Let's put aside the fact that the conference costs five hundred dollars per person."

Ezra and I look at each other. I reach into a pocket and pull out my phone, which has a little wallet magnetized to the back.

"I've got twenty dollars," I say, fishing out the crumpled bill. "I was going to use it at next week's field trip to the Natural History museum, but, you know . . ."

Ezra reaches into his suit jacket pocket and pulls out a sealed envelope. "From my uncle Chaim," he explains, opening the envelope and removing a card.

On the outside cover, the card has a picture of a smiling tortilla chip, underneath the words "Much nachos on your bar mitzvah!" Inside, the chip has put on a yarmulke and the message reads, "Just kidding! Much nachas! (And nachos!)"

"Your uncle Chaim's hilarious," I say, reading over Ezra's shoulder.

Ezra groans. "Is he?"

There's also a handwritten addition on the card that reads, "Love you, Ezra!" More important, the envelope comes with a check, which I snatch from Ezra's hand and slide across the table, along with my cash.

I wink at the registration lady. "Don't suppose you'd take twenty dollars and"—I glance at the check and sigh—"and a check for another eighteen made out to Ezra's parents?"

She gently pushes the money back toward me. "The main issue is that registration for the conference closed on Friday." She chuckles to herself again. "You'd basically have to go back in time two days and register then."

Ezra and I give polite smiles. "We'll do that, ma'am,"

I say, yanking Ezra away. "Thanks so much for your help."

"Slight hiccup," I tell Ezra. "Nothing we can't handle. I know you don't like to skip school on Loop-Friday. But I think it would be best if we meet back here first thing that morning."

"Okay, but—"

"Great. It's gonna make the whole loop a bit of a nightmare for me—my parents really dig the usual Friday morning rituals—but I'll bike straight to the hotel as soon as I wake up. Leave a note for them or something. They'll be okay. We should scout the conference as soon as possible."

"Fine, but—"

"Oh, shoot. Let's grab one of those schedules. Maybe there's a list of scientists who we can research online. Figure out who's most likely to have accidentally busted up the fabric of space-time."

"Finn!" Ezra shouts, stepping in front of me, stopping me in my tracks. "What about the money?"

I squint at him. "What about it?"

"Even if we register on Friday, we still need *a thousand dollars* to get inside."

I smile, pat his shoulder. "You're worried about the money? That part's gonna be easy. We're stuck in a time loop, remember? I've been waiting for an excuse to try."

Now *there's* that classic Ezra *What the heck are you talking about?* face. "Do I even want to know?"

I say nothing, just to build the suspense.

"You're going to make me ask, aren't you?" he says.

I bat my eyelashes, sway back and forth, stay silent.

"Ugh, fine. *Finn*, pretty please tell me. What have you been waiting to try?"

I smile, give it another few seconds, then let him have it.

"Why, winning the lottery of course."

★ 11 ★

EZRA

Let's win the lottery, Finn says.

It's going to be easy, Finn says.

Finn says a lot of things.

I mean, it's a decent idea. It *is* easy to know all the winning numbers. It's everything else that's hard, like: Turns out they don't sell lottery tickets to kids. And the guy behind the gas station counter does not accept "but we're both bar mitzvah boys!" as valid proof of adulthood under New Jersey state law.

So we try every grown-up we know.

Finn's parents. Nope. My parents. Double nope. Rabbi Neumann refuses to consider the request, asking if we're "instead interested in the biggest grand prize there is—learning!" Andy Pauli literally chases us out of the Bergenville lobby. And then Finn insists (and insists and insists) that we "ask the boldest, baddest eighteen-year-old around." One who doesn't mind breaking rules, getting in trouble.

"Please, no," I say.

"Come on," Finn urges. "Trust me, once we have a ticket in hand, *the rest* will be easy."

"Go away!" Avital shouts from inside her room.

I knock again. "Please open the door. I need a favor."

"Take the bus. Or ask Abba to drive you. I can't today. I'm busy."

"It's not that. And don't you have school?"

"Don't *you* have school?"

"Please open up, Avital. You're my favorite big sister."

"Not falling for it."

"I'll be your best friend?"

"Pass."

"*Please*. It's my bar mitzvah weekend. You know Imma and Abba are going to ignore me the whole time. Don't you want to help me celebrate my special day?"

Silence. And then the door unlocks.

"Cheap shot," Avital says, letting me in.

I'm hit with the usual pang of jealousy. Avital's the

only sibling with her own room. Something about being the oldest. If Finn and I ever escape the time loop, Avital will graduate high school in May, and then I'll get my own room too. I'm hoping it'll be this one. It isn't big. But it's still got a lot going for it. It's at the end of the upstairs hallway, farthest from our parents' room. It's got its own door leading into the bathroom all us kids share. And—unlike mine and Eitan's room, or Esty and Eliana's—Avital's window lets out above the sloped first-floor roof, out of sight of the living room windows. Perfect for sneaking, which Avital has been taking full advantage of.

"What do you want?" she asks.

Her voice is strange. She looks upset. And like every Saturday night—when she steals the car—she's wearing a coat over her clothes, even though it's not cold out. "Why are you acting weird?" I ask.

Avital crosses her arms. "Do you need something or not?"

I take a breath. No way to ask other than to ask. "I need you to drive me and a friend to the gas station on West Pinewood and buy us a lottery ticket *right now*."

Avital blinks at me for a few seconds, then bursts out laughing. "Why would I do that?"

"Because you're a good sister?"

"Try again."

"Because it's my bar mitzvah?"

"That was the price of admission into my room. It's not getting me to run your very bizarre errand." She starts shoving things into her backpack. A change of clothes. A crumpled hat. A set of keys I don't recognize. "Why do you even want a lottery ticket? It's a waste of money you don't have."

"I was hoping you'd let me borrow some."

"You're not serious."

I point to her wallet, which is lying open on her bed. There's cash spilling out from one of the pockets.

"You've got enough. A lottery ticket's only like two dollars. I'll pay you back. I promise. Either from the winnings or the eighteen-dollar check Uncle Chaim gives me at the party on Sunday."

Avital sighs. "Uncle Chaim, huh? Man of the hour. You sure he's *also* giving you a check?"

Right. How *am* I supposed to know that? I scramble. "Um, doesn't he give everyone eighteen-dollar checks for everything?"

She accepts this. "Fine. But I'm still not lending you a cent for the lottery. It's throwing money in the garbage. No way." Avital snaps her wallet shut, throws it in her backpack with everything else. "Nope. Sorry! Now get out of my room so I can get ready."

She starts closing the door in my face, and I consider the options. I like Avital. She helps me with my homework sometimes and doesn't hate playing Stratego with me on Shabbos afternoon, and she once covered for me when I totally left Imma's car lights on and the batteries died—even though I was the last one out of the car and everyone told me not to forget to turn them off. She's a good big sister. I have no complaints. Which is why this next bit is so hard.

"If you don't buy me a lottery ticket, I'm going to tell Abba about Saturday night."

Inches away from closed, the door creaks back open. "Excuse me?"

"I feel awful about this," I say. "And I don't need to know the details. I respect your privacy, which is why I've never asked. It doesn't matter what you're doing. You could have a secret boyfriend for all I care."

Avital's eyes go wide, and I can't help myself: "Wait. Do you have a secret boyfriend? Is it Reuven Rothwax from Bnei Baruch? Please tell me it's not Reuven Rothwax from Bnei Baruch. Gross."

Avital doesn't say a word, so I back up: "You know what? Forget I asked. I hope you and Reuven are very happy together. And I won't tell Abba. I swear. *If* you help me."

Avital's face is redder than a pomegranate. She's breathing slow and heavy. Her hands are balled into fists. She's never been an "I'll beat you up" kind of sister. But I guess there's a first time loop for everything. Five seconds go by. Ten.

Her shoulders droop. "I thought I was your favorite big sister."

"You are!" I give her a hug, so she knows I mean it. "The favoritest."

Avital worms out of my arms.

"You are so weird, you know that?" Avital says, and then she grabs a set of car keys from her desk and leads me out to the driveway.

There are lots of lotteries, for lots of prizes. But most of them announce winning numbers *at night*, which doesn't work for us. Thursday night is too early, pre-loop. Saturday night is too late—we're trying to make it in time to register for the whole weekend. And Friday night is Shabbos. No go. We need a *daytime* lottery, and when Avital drives me and Finn to the gas station early Friday morning—there's only one choice. A single game that we can still buy tickets for, with numbers announced Friday at 10:00 a.m.: the Northeast Superball. Winning numbers: 1, 7, 12, 13, 40, 70 (weekly "doubler": 49).

Grand prize . . .

"Two hundred fifty-seven million dollars?!" I scream, staring at the neon display. It's a hilarious amount of money. "What do we need two hundred fifty-seven million dollars for?!"

"Go big or go back in time," Finn says.

"That doesn't *mean* anything," I grumble as we call Avital over. She uses the little multiple-choice scantron and a tiny pencil. Enters the Superball and waits with us, even though we tell her not to.

"I do not understand what's gotten into you." She points at Finn. "Or who this kid is. But I'm not leaving you guys alone at a gas station." She even buys us sodas and chips for breakfast, which makes me feel even worse for how I treated her. "You owe me one, big-time."

"For sure," I agree. "You can have half the money. All of it, really. I just need a thousand bucks."

Avital slumps down onto the curb and starts scrolling on her phone. "Yeah, sure, whatever. Let me know when we can get out of here."

And then the winning numbers go live, and everything kind of falls apart.

At exactly ten o'clock, I ask Avital to refresh the lottery website, which she does—glancing at her phone, glancing at our ticket, glancing at her phone, glancing at our ticket—before nearly passing out. Finn and I have to help her to her feet and splash ice-cold Mountain Dew in her face. When she finally gets herself together, she figures "this must be some kind of mistake," and goes into the gas station to clear everything up. But the attendant behind the counter screams at the top of his lungs that, yes, we did just win *257 million dollars*, and Avital nearly passes out again. (This time we wake her up with Finn's Dr Pepper, because I'd finished the last of my drink.) And that's when things *really* spiral out of control. Shaking, tears rolling down her cheeks, despite us begging her not to, Avital calls Imma and Abba. Someone calls a news crew. And the two other people wandering the little gas station market appear to call everyone they have ever met. In minutes, it's a zoo. People are cheering. Avital is weeping. Microphones in our faces—

"How does it feel to be millionaires overnight?"

"What are you going to do with the winnings?"

"How did you choose the numbers?"

Only Finn talks to the cameras, hands on his hips, all confidence. "We were feeling lucky is all. And it's barely even two hundred mil after taxes, you know?" He turns. "Get my good side!"

And then my parents show up, and Finn's parents show up, and they drag us out of the gas station, driving straight to a drab lawyer's office on the other side of town. Finn and I keep trying to see if we can "please get a little of the money right now?" But our parents ignore the request and lock us in a waiting room for the rest of the day.

I don't make it back to the Bergenville. My parents cancel the whole bar mitzvah. And it's not the worst weekend I've ever had? But we're no richer at the end of it, and 1:36 p.m. comes and goes.

"In retrospect," Finn says, the next Loop-Friday around, "we should have known that, like, the gas station guy couldn't open the register and hand us two hundred fifty-seven million dollars cash."

"You think?" I say. We're back at the gas station, waiting for them to announce today's Quick 4. Winning numbers: 5, 9, 16, 17. Grand prize for the week: a less newsworthy $973.

"It'll work this time," Finn declares.

And of course it doesn't.

No one faints when we go to trade in the ticket. But the cashier won't give us our thousand dollars either. We have to "mail the ticket to the lottery commission, then wait three to six weeks," which may as well be instructions to "mail the ticket to the lottery commission, then wait three to six centuries."

Avital's impressed anyway. "Okay, this is pretty cool." But she still has somewhere to be, taps her foot, and goes, "Can we leave now?"

Next.

"Forget the lottery," Finn says, holding up his parents' credit card. "We should have just started here."

But the lady at the registration table "needs to see some identification, young man." And no matter how much Finn looks like his dad, we can't ever convince her that Finn is Leo Dylan Einstein, six feet two inches, age thirty-nine.

Next.

"New plan," Finn says, tapping at the library computer screen, googling around for new ideas. "We get Avital to bet on this horse race happening down in Ocean County. Rules say it pays out right after the race. Last one on Friday is at two p.m. Okay?"

Okay. And we do it—win an actual prize after a horse named Kaleidoscope runs a mile in less than two minutes. But instead of sharing, Avital pockets all $2,200 in cash, ignores us the whole ride back home, and refuses to give us a cent.

✦ ✦ ✦

Next.

"All right," Finn says. "I'm thinking Avital is the wrong approach." He spreads a copy of *The Bergenville Gazette* out in my front driveway, opening to the familiar events page. "Karaoke contest. Grand prize: One thousand dollars. It's perfect."

But we're horrible. One of the guys in the audience complains that "those kids should pay *us* a thousand dollars for having to listen to that." And we lose to two grandmas singing Bruce Springsteen at the top of their lungs.

Next.

"What if we sell something?" Finn tries again. "Do your parents have any jewelry to pawn?"

And I know I shouldn't. Even if they'll never remember, even if everything resets anyway, *I shouldn't*. But my head is spinning, and Finn insists (and insists and insists), so I do it. I swipe my mom's engagement ring, and we go to sell it at the store on Cypress Lane—

Where the cashier behind the counter calls my parents, because I have the worst luck in the world. They all know each other from the school PTA. And Imma and

Abba show up even angrier than that time they called the police on me.

"How could you?" my mom asks, cold and quiet. "We do *everything* for you. And you steal? You're a thief now? We raised a thief? Are things really that bad?"

"Of all weekends," my father says, not looking me in the eye. "You chose this one?"

"Okay," Finn says, pacing my living room. "Don't say no until you've heard me out. What about"—he extends his arms, fingers splayed—"a time-loop bank heist."

My jaw falls open. "No!" I scream. Then I shriek in Finn's face and storm out the front door.

I can't take it anymore. I don't tell anyone where I'm going. I don't even know myself. Not at first. I just hop on my bike, and my legs take me there. Across the neighborhood. Through downtown. To the Bergenville.

"You cannot leave your bicycle there!" Andy Pauli orders as I enter the lobby, pointing to where I ditched the bike. He moves to block me, stands in my way. "Also, no running in the hotel. And—"

"Not now!" I shout, shoving past him, through the corridors, to the main convention hall at the rear of the hotel.

"Can I help—" the woman at the registration table starts to say.

I slap her stupid placard off the table. Then I feel bad and pick it back up, try to flatten out a crease I made in the side, return it to its place.

"Sorry. That was rude. Sorry. But I don't get it. You're scientists. Why make admission so expensive? How are students supposed to learn if they need a thousand dollars to get inside?! Why can't we just go in?!"

She blinks at me politely, pointing to one of the dozen flyers in front of her. "Well, we do have a student rate."

My stomach drops through the floor. "Student rate?"

She smiles. "We're so happy to welcome interested, curious attendees into the conference. I'll need to see a student ID and"—she eyes the flyer—"eighteen dollars."

I'm suddenly sweating and freezing all at once. I can feel my hands shaking, my heart racing. My brain feels like it's about to explode.

I spin around, shouting at the whole room, "WHY DIDN'T YOU TELL US THAT IN THE FIRST PLACE?!"

The woman looks confused, leans away from me, touches a hand to her chest. "I'm sorry," she says kindly. "Have we met before?"

12

FINN

"How'd you get in here?"

I stand up straight and begin: "Dr. London? You don't know us, but we know you. I'm Finn. This is my friend Ezra. We're trapped in a time loop, and we need your help."

One Mississippi. Two Mississippi. Three Mississippi.

"Ha!" She cranes to see around us. "Okay! Who put you up to this? Carl? You back there? Very funny."

I think Ezra's still mad at me. Who could blame him—some of my ideas were real stinkers. Of course, this whole thing is trial and error. But I get it. We could have skipped a few runs. And as resident time-loop expert, I take full responsibility. My bad. I'm making up for it though. And we've got this next part moving like clockwork.

I hold out a hand. Ezra slaps the first three-by-five index card into my open palm, the message written in Sharpie: "Carl?" the index card reads. "You back there? Very funny."

Dr. London takes the card, adjusts her glasses. "What is this? I don't have time for this."

Ezra silently passes me the second card in the stack. I hand it to Dr. London. She reads it out loud: "What is this? I don't have time for this."

We've scoured every inch of the thirty-seventh annual Mid-Atlantic Conference of Interdisciplinary Quantum Physicists. Poked our heads into every room. Sat in on a dozen presentations. And nothing. There are no hidden particle accelerators. No tiny tokomaks. As best we can tell, there are no experiments going on here at all. Nothing *happens* at 1:36 p.m. to trigger the loop. Nothing explodes or sparks or so much as glows at Reset. Instead, at that exact moment, all the attendees are in the main hall, listening to the most boring speech of the whole conference. One second, IQP vice chair and treasurer JoAnn Halban is talking about "the upcoming board vote to add a new associate tier of membership for non-doctorate university faculty," and the next, I'm back in my bed on Friday morning.

"It's nice to meet you kids," Dr. London says, lifting her laptop screen. "But I've got a busy day ahead. Don't make me call security."

Dr. Jamie London is kind of a rock star around here—or what passes for a rock star at a physics convention. For one thing, she's got this office to herself. Monday through Thursday, pre-loop, it's some boring "Bergenville Sales Team Business Center." But this weekend, it's all Dr. London's. A place for her to camp out between events. Type entire math textbooks into that computer right there. She's on a dozen panels. Is one of the conference's "keynote speakers." And her main event—a solo talk on "The Frontier of Temporal Mechanics"—is standing room only.

If anyone can help us, it's her.

Ezra passes me the third card: "But I've got a busy day ahead. Please don't make me call security."

I wince, because Dr. London didn't use "Please" this loop around. Ezra and I try to behave the same with her, every time. An accidental squint, a sneeze, an extra step to the left or right—anything can nudge the loop out of whack. Luckily, this variant of Dr. London doesn't seem to care that our card was slightly more polite than she was.

She stands. "Anyone would say that," Dr. London says, back on script.

"Test us," Ezra insists.

Dr. London looks from him, to me, and back, just like always. And just like always, a small grin appears at the edges of her mouth. "Pineapple pizza," she says, winking.

Ezra materializes a new card: "Pineapple pizza." A little winky-face emoji in the corner.

Her eyes go wide, and then she sings the ABCs in reverse order. Ezra hands her a card that reads, "ABCs."

"Aha!" She pumps a fist. "That's not what I—"

"Turn it over," I say.

And she does, revealing the word: "Backward."

Dr. London takes a deep breath and exhales. She runs her hands through her hair, presses her fingers into her eyes. Then she begins patting at her desk—finding a pen, clicking it open, and writing a formula on the back of a Bergenville Hotel–branded napkin: "$h = 6.62607015 \times 10^{-34}$ J·Hz^{-1}."

We hand her the next card, where we've written this

exact formula—plus little smiley faces I drew inside the zeros.

Dr. London peers down and gasps. The cards spill from her hands to the floor, and she collapses into her desk chair. "You're trapped in a time loop," she says.

Ezra and I look at each other. "And we need your help," Ezra adds. "*Please.*"

The doctor slowly nods, raises her gaze to us. "What happens now?" she asks.

I take a step forward. "We don't know. I mean, we know *out there*." I gesture to my sides, at the hotel, the world. "We've run our loop more times than either of us can count. But we don't know what happens *in here*. Whether you'll help us or not. Whether you can. This is as far as we've gotten with you. That was our last card."

Ezra holds up his empty hands to prove the point.

Dr. London nods again. She understands. "I mean, it's always been conceivable," she says. "But we're so far from understanding temporal disruptions on a quantum level that don't interfere with self-consistent solutions. To align transmission and reception events with any kind of universal simultaneity . . . I mean, sure, Angela and I joke about tachyonic antitelephones, but I don't even want to think about the paradox that would flow from all the MWI disruptions you—"

"Hey, Doc?" I say.

She blinks at me, waiting.

"Can you help us?"

Dr. London sits up straight, determination on her face, then fear, then wonder, then absolute joy. She flips the napkin over to the other side and clicks her pen again.

"Tell me everything."

13

EZRA

"Paris?"

"No."

"Disney World."

"No."

It's the fourth or fifth loop since bringing Dr. London onboard. She says she's making progress. Finn believes her. But who knows? It's slow work. Hard to do science when you keep forgetting why you're doing it.

Every Friday morning, Finn and I run our card game in Dr. London's office. We tell her about the loop, convince her to help us, *and* explain that she already has. And every Sunday afternoon, before my bar mitzvah speech, we meet up with her again. She has us memorize a few words or numbers—an equation here, a subatomic particle there. Something new to tell her on the next loop. Little "head starts," which help Dr. London get further with her work each weekend around.

A few times, Dr. London scanned us with this little beeping device she borrowed from a colleague. Last loop, she pricked our fingertips and took samples of blood. Once, she brought us up in front of the whole conference, told them our story, pretended we were part of some "thought experiment."

"Imagine you've been tasked with unsticking these young men in time," she said to all the other scientists, flipping a whiteboard where she'd scrawled endless math. "Here's what we already know. What would you do from here?"

But mostly, she works alone, leaving me and Finn free to, well—

"Empire State Building," he suggests. "Can we at least go to the top of the Empire State Building?"

"No!" I say. "What about school? What about my bar mitzvah?"

Finn crosses his arms. "Since when do you care about any of that?"

It's not the worst point he's ever made. But what am

I supposed to tell him? That we can't risk messing with the flow of Dr. London's work? That I've had enough pointless Finn Einstein adventures for one life? That I don't think I can take getting lost or caught or arrested or whatever, and having to add yet another image of my family's heartbroken faces to my collection?

Actually, that all sounds pretty good in my head. I repeat it out loud to Finn. Naturally, he doesn't care.

"Come on," he whines. "We're not doing anything anymore. We deserve a vacation loop."

"So go," I say, heading toward the closest hotel exit. It's Friday morning. We just finished up with Dr. London. "Enjoy. I'll see you Sunday."

Finn walks backward in front of me, following me out. "Nooo! It'll be boring alone. *Please.* Anything, whatever you want, we can do anything."

I stop. Finn stops. He smiles. I smile.

"Anything?" I ask.

Finn rubs his palms together. "Anything."

Before I can ring the bell, Finn's dad opens their front door wide.

"Come in, come in!" he says, tilting his head behind him. "Finn! Your friend is here!"

Finn comes trudging down the steps. "When I said *anything*, I meant, like, Stonehenge or the Great Wall of China or whatever."

It's Loop-Saturday night, after the end of Shabbos. I asked Avital to drop me here on her way out and told my parents I was sleeping at Dovi's. (An excuse I already know works well enough.) Because Paris? Disney World? *Stonehenge?* Nope. There's only one place in the whole world I want to see.

"Congrats! Finn tells us it's your bar mitzvah too," his mom calls from the living room couch, beneath a wood-carved sign that reads, "Home Sweet Home."

"Thanks, Mrs. E!" I say back, which is always what she tells me to call her whenever we meet for the first time. It isn't like I haven't interacted with his mom and dad before. But I still don't quite get Finn's whole attitude. His parents are amazing, so what's he always complaining about? And why have we spent a million runs in *my* loop but none in his?

Finn leads me to the already-set kitchen table while his dad steps over to the couch and leans down.

"Shall we?" he asks Finn's mom, who smiles and takes his arm.

They're so sweet. She's always leaning on him. He's

always offering to get her stuff. I've never once seen them fight. Not to be confused with a certain other family I know.

"Pizza's hot!" Finn's dad says, delivering the boxes to the table.

And dinner's perfect. Finn's parents ordered from Naphtali's, my absolute favorite kosher pizza place. And everyone's eating off paper plates, using plastic cutlery.

"I don't mind if you use your regular dishes," I say. Just because I only eat off kosher plates doesn't mean I need them to do the same.

Finn's mom waves me down. "Nonsense. We're delighted to have a friend of Finn's over and are happy to accommodate as best we can."

Finn groans like his mom said the opposite of something perfectly nice.

"Besides," Finn's dad adds, holding up a spicy fry, "I think I may have found *my* new favorite pizza place."

I laugh. He laughs. Finn's mom laughs. This *is* a nice vacation.

"So, Ezra," Finn's dad says. "Finn tells us you two met because you're both stuck in a time loop."

I nearly drop the slice in my lap, until Finn's dad starts laughing again and his mom adds, "Doesn't our

Finny have the *best* imagination?"

Finn cracks a smile. He sticks out his tongue at his dad, who throws a spicy fry across the table. Finn manages to bite it out of the air, to his dad's thunderous applause. Then Finn takes a few tiny bows as his mom stares at them both with wide glassy eyes like she has never seen anything so beautiful. Sure, I can't remember the last time I saw my parents look at me that way. But I also can't remember the last time I saw *anyone* look at *anyone* that way.

Finn's mom dabs her eyes with a napkin, then gently places it back down onto the table. "I'll clean up."

Finn's dad shoots up from his chair. "I got it, I got it. You relax. Sit with the kids."

She rolls her eyes but allows Mr. Einstein to start collecting plates into the empty pizza box.

"Is it always like this?" I whisper to Finn.

"Like what?"

Ice cream for dessert, with cups of tea all around. ("Finn," his mom teases. "It's tea with honey, remember? Not honey with tea.") A little TV (rewatching half a time-loop movie Finn's already made me sit through like six times). And then bed, in Finn's own room, his own everything.

I'm lying on a trundle they pulled out from underneath Finn's bed. He's on his back, staring up at the ceiling, hands behind his head. It's quiet for a while, and then Finn breaks the silence.

"'Tomorrow, and tomorrow, and tomorrow,'" he says in a low voice, "'creeps in this petty pace from day to day.'" He stops, waits for me to recite the next line.

To the last syllable of recorded time, I think, but say nothing, mostly to annoy him.

"What's that from?" I ask.

He jolts up, slaps his forehead. "*What?!* It's Shakespeare! *Macbeth!*" What we're covering in language arts class. "We've been over this. So many times. Come on!"

I smile and go—"That's a little too much *sound and fury* for this hour, don't you think?"—referencing a later line in the speech.

He collapses back onto his bed. "*Lighted fool*," he says, referencing another line.

It's quiet again for another minute, maybe two.

"What're you gonna do when you get out?" Finn eventually asks.

My favorite question. And my least favorite. It's all I can think about, sometimes. Imagine the future, even though it feels like I'll never get there.

"There's a sleepaway yeshiva in Buffalo," I tell him. "Some eighth graders I know went there for high school this year. I've always thought I'd leave home after twelfth grade. But maybe I can go earlier. Not like I haven't put in the time at home."

Finn nods. "I totally get it. I'm going to double down too. Straight A's. Extracurriculars. As many AP classes as possible once I get to high school. Maybe I'll be able to graduate early. College at seventeen, or something like that. Never look back."

I point to a framed photo on the wall—his parents holding toddler-Finn up by the hands, swinging him into the air, their faces wall-to-wall smiles. "*This* is the family you're trying to escape?"

"It's not all fairies and unicorns," Finn says.

"Sure seems like it."

Finn sits up again. "Well, then, it's fairies and unicorns, but they're way too perfect and are constantly throwing pixie dust *everywhere* while you can't even get, like, a single forest gnome to want to come to your bar mitzvah."

I sit up too. "Huh?"

Finn exhales through puffed-up cheeks. "Grass is always greener in the other loop, I guess. Besides, you're one to talk."

"What do you mean?"

"You're always complaining too, even though your family is so fun and wild and *real* and you have more friends than you know what to do with."

"I do not."

He shakes his head. "You don't even know what you have."

"Grass is always greener in the other loop," I repeat. But I don't feel like arguing. "I'm going to the bathroom," I say. "Door across the hall, right?"

"Or at the far end. We've got two up here, not including the one in my parents' room."

I roll my eyes, step into the hallway, and close the door behind me.

I breathe in deep and exhale. It's so quiet in this house. The floorboards creak with every step. You can hear the crickets chirping outside. You can never hear anything in my own house—except running or yelling or door slamming. I walk down the hallway, deciding to go to the farther bathroom after all, take advantage of the peace. Man, Finn is so—

I hear a sound through a nearby wall, behind a closed door. It's coming from inside Finn's parents' bedroom. And it's a sound I recognize. Like the running, like the yelling, like the door slamming—it's a sound that belongs in *my* house, not Finn's. Someone is sniffling. Someone is *crying*.

"It's okay," a voice says, too low for me to tell if it's Finn's mom or dad.

I glance both ways, toward the opposite ends of the hallway. It feels like I'm doing something wrong, like I'm eavesdropping, even though I don't mean to—

Until I do.

"We should tell him," a voice whispers. Finn's dad? No, mom.

"Why? We don't know anything for sure. What's the point? Let's wait until after we get the car."

"The point is so he *knows*." That's definitely Finn's mom. But who is *he*? And knows *what*? Finn says he's run perfect loops. Could he have gotten there without figuring out his own family?

"Can we talk about this another day?" one of them says.

The other sighs. "We've had this conversation a hundred times. It's always *another day*."

"Tomorrow. Please. Let's just wait until after tomorrow."

And tomorrow, and tomorrow, I think.

They don't say anything after that. Or at least I don't hear them. So I use the bathroom—replaying the conversation in my mind—and return to Finn's room. I close the door behind me, heart pounding. Why is my heart pounding? Inside my head, I hear Finn's voice: *There's something here. Something wrong. Something to fix.*

I tell Finn what I heard.

"Yeah," he says. "They think I don't know we're getting a new car on Tuesday, post-loop. Obviously I found out. Sure, I liked our old car, but whatever. Times change. Not a big deal."

"I don't know," I say. "I think something might be . . . off. Wrong."

"Well *you're* wrong," he snaps, flipping to his side, turning toward the wall. "And one sleepover doesn't make you an expert in my life."

"I never said it did."

"Forget it. Sorry. I'm tired." He pulls the covers up over his shoulder. "Let's just go to bed and focus on tomorrow, okay?"

★ 14 ★

FINN

But tomorrow isn't better.

"I can't do it," Dr. London tells us the next morning, her head low. We're back in her office. "I can't fix you. Not like this."

"What do you mean?" I ask. "You *have* to."

She shakes her head. "I *might* be starting to understand what's happening here. Tachyon readings on anything you two touch are through the roof. I've never encountered that kind of non-bradyonic incidence, even on a theoretical level. No clue *why* you are the way you are. But there's a chance—a *chance*—I can synthesize some kind of . . . antidote."

"That sounds . . . good?" Ezra says. "Great!"

"It's not *anything*, unless I can study it further."

"So study it," I beg.

"I can't. Not really. I keep *forgetting* everything. Starting every loop from scratch."

"But you're not starting from scratch," Ezra reminds her. "You have the head starts."

"They're not enough anymore. I need to maintain my *entire* dataset from one loop to the next."

"Great," I say. "No problem. We'll remember it. We can do it."

We're seated around Dr. London's desk, Ezra and me on one side, Dr. London on the other. She reaches forward and turns her laptop around. The screen is covered in math, like someone took all the numbers in the world, mixed them up, and spilled them into a single spreadsheet. Dozens of columns. Endless rows. Formulas in each cell. She clicks to scroll down, and down, and down. It's a bottomless pit of digits and signs and that uppercase "E" that looks more like a stretched-out "M" on its side.

"You'll remember all this?" Dr. London asks.

Ezra slumps down into his chair, stretches his neck backward. "Another dead end," he says.

"No," I say, sitting up straight. "No. It can't be. We're stuck in a *time loop* in the same hotel as a *time scientist*."

Dr. London raises a hand. "Technically, my PhD is in theoretical quant—"

I keep talking. "It *can't* be a coincidence, which means this *has to* be the solution, which means there's a way to get you the data you need. Take it with us from Sunday back to Friday."

"How?" Ezra asks. "You know we can't keep things from one loop to the next. We've tried everything."

Dr. London bolts up from her seat. "You haven't tried everything," she says, picking up her computer. She detaches the screen, puts the keyboard down, and begins pacing the room, typing and speaking at the speed of light.

"It shouldn't work. I mean, it *doesn't* work. But we don't need to send signals into the future, only the past, which takes care of one problem. We only need one-way communication, which takes care of another. And you're both already screaming off tachyons like there's no tomorrow." She pauses and looks up. "Sorry." Then she gets back to it, typing, typing, typing: "Loop-Sunday is A. Loop-Friday is B. It's not rocket science. Per the Lorentz transformation, at least some values of v can make delta t negative, and the effect arises before the cause!"

Dr. London freezes in place, her back to us. Then she spins around, holding out the screen like Eliana Rosen showing off her latest LEGO creation.

"Ta-da!" Dr. London cheers.

Ezra and I lean forward. "More numbers?" Ezra points out.

Dr. London peers over the screen, then runs a single finger down the center, scrolling to the bottom. There's a graph sitting beneath the new data.

"Ta-da!" she says again.

It's an image of a line, starting near Dr. London's right hand, reaching toward her left. It runs across the screen, then up—before bending backward on itself, curving down, starting over. I recognize the shape. I've made them myself. I *live* them.

It's a loop.

Dr. London smiles. "I can't believe I'm saying this, but I might be able to craft a rudimentary tachyonic antitelephone. We're only sending *data*, which I can convert to a quantum state from here. And given that you two are the only ones caught in this loop, there shouldn't be too much collateral damage."

"What does any of that mean?" Ezra asks.

She opens a drawer, fishes around, and pulls out a small thumb drive. "It means that, with the right adjustments, I should be able to set this little guy up to travel back with you. I'll record a video of myself, catch me up to speed, and include *all* the data I've compiled, compounding my research with every loop. The drive should stay in its drawer from the end of one loop to the beginning of the next. Don't want to risk too much causal distortion. But it should meet us here every Friday, data intact." She pauses. "Theoretically."

I still don't understand every detail, but I understand enough. "A teeny-tiny time machine."

Dr. London nods. "A teeny-tiny time machine."

Ezra is beaming. "That's amazing. Thank you. Let's do it."

I close my eyes for a moment, allow myself to see into the future just around the corner. My first job. College. High school. *Monday.*

So much possibility. Almost there.

I open my eyes, as Dr. London's face falls.

"One last problem," she says. "This conference is still mostly a conference. There are some materials here that I can use. But to finish the job, I need sufficient Faraday caging. I could probably get ahold of aluminum mesh or copper wire in the time I have, but those aren't ideal materials, and we don't want the data leaking out from one loop to the next. Bad data would be worse than none at all."

"Whatever you need, Doc," I say. "Anything."

"What I *need* is a kilo of palladium, or maybe two dozen gold bars. I don't suppose you kids are heirs to a crate of pirate treasure?"

"We are not," I say, already pondering ways to make ourselves heirs to a crate of pirate treasure.

My head spins with ideas. But Ezra won't agree to any of them. His eyes are down, his lips pursed. He doesn't have the stomach for some new scheme? Fine. Alone it is. I grab my knees, ready to stand and announce that I'll take care of everything, as usual. That Ezra can go home, live his loop in peace. That I'll return once I've gotten Dr. London what she needs.

Ezra stands first. "Time-loop bank heist?" he asks, voice steady, eyes set straight ahead.

I slowly rise to my feet. Those words, out of Ezra Rosen's mouth. "I thought you'd never ask."

★ 15 ★

EZRA

"Run!" Finn screams through the pods in my ear. "Get out of there!"

I scramble to my feet—not too fast, don't want to draw attention—and hop down the fire escape, dropping hard to the sidewalk. Why did I suggest this again?

"What about you?" I mutter under my breath. I shake myself off, make my way toward Penn Station, walking slow like everything's perfectly normal.

"Forget about me," Finn says. He's down the block. Getting farther away with every step I take. "I'm cornered. I'll see you on the next loop. Save yourself. But this was good. I got the intel. I promise. We just need one more run."

"Yeah, I've heard that bef—"

I'm cut off by the sound of a struggle, a "Stop right there!" and a "Hey! Let go of me!" Then Finn cuts the connection, and I'm alone.

"That makes nine tries," I say the next Friday around. We're on the sidewalk in front of my house.

"You know what I always say," Finn responds, plucking a stick off the curb. "Tenth loop's the charm!"

"You have never said that."

He shrugs, and starts drawing in the dirt patch surrounding the tree in my front yard. One line, two, four. A large box. The bank.

"It's not to scale," Finn says, "X" marking the spot. "Vault is here. We know they've got the gold inside."

We started by staking out as many tristate area banks as possible. Which ones have safety-deposit vaults? Which vaults are visited by customers on Loop-Friday? Which customers withdraw gold bars?

It was a ton of work all to find one person.

"Chandler Pog," Finn continues, drawing a stick figure in the dirt. Finn scratches in a little bow tie. It's not a bad likeness.

The real-life Chandler Pog wears a three-piece suit, red button-down shirt, cell phone glued to his ear. Every

Loop-Friday, he visits a midtown bank for ten minutes and leaves with $30,000 in gold bars.

"Getting to the vault isn't the hard part," Finn continues, drawing arrows, marking rooms.

He's right. It took a few loops. But Finn's been successfully following Mr. Pog to the back of the bank for a while. It didn't work to—

Just ask him if we can come along. (My idea. After the "we have a student rate" debacle, I'm not forgetting to try the easy approach.)

Crawl through the air ducts and drop in through the ceiling. (Finn's idea. He never got close to the vault *and* broke a leg in the process.)

Impersonate Mr. Pog. (Neither one of us can pull off the fake mustache.)

Here's what works: Waiting for Mr. Pog to follow a security guard into the vault—one, two, three seconds—before one of us runs into the bank and asks the branch assistant manager Charlotte Moyal if "Grandpa is already in the vault? Oh no! I'm late and so sorry can I please go back there I was supposed to meet him here fifteen minutes ago and he's gonna be so mad at me if I don't catch up so we can look at my parents' old wedding rings together because I'm an orphan and because they died and because because because—"

Cue tears.

A sniffle or two.

It has to be three seconds (no more, no less). It can only be one of us (not both). And it has to be Charlotte Moyal. (The other tellers pick up the interoffice phone and call the vault to fetch Mr. Pog, ruining the whole thing.)

In front of my house, Finn moves on, still adding to his schematic as he talks.

"It really is the perfect place to wait," he says, tracing a path from the bank lobby, through the vault doors. There are bathrooms back there, and a small alcove near the vault, where he hid on the last loop. "I was so close."

"Then what happened?" I ask. "Was it the briefcase?" A replica of the one Mr. Pog uses to store his withdrawal. We packed it with rocks from my yard and LEGO bricks from Eliana's room, working hard to get the weight just right. Finn is supposed to swap it out for the real thing without Mr. Pog noticing.

"No. The briefcase was perfect."

"You made the switch?"

"Yeah! The plan worked amazing. I waited until he was done in the vault and bumped into him as he was heading out—hard enough to knock the case out of his hand like we practiced. In the commotion, I managed to kick the real briefcase into the alcove behind me and trade it for the fake. He took it and left."

I whistle. "Impressive."

"Eh," Finn continues. "He left . . . until he didn't. I waited three minutes"—the usual amount of time it takes Mr. Pog to leave the bank and get to his car—"but something about the crash in the hallway makes him into a more careful version of himself. He never double-checked the briefcase before. This time, he didn't leave the bank right away. He paused here"—Finn makes a new mark in the dirt—"and checked on the gold before exiting."

"No! What did he do when he found the LEGO bricks?"

"It's worse than that," Finn says. "He didn't just find them. He opened the briefcase and spilled them all out onto the floor. They went everywhere."

"I thought you secured them in the case!"

"I did! But dropping the briefcase in the corridor must have knocked them loose. There he was, shouting on his phone, staring at a dozen rocks and a thousand shiny pointy LEGO gems, instead of gold."

"Wait—you used the *gems*? I thought we were going with the plain bricks."

"We were," Finn says. "But last minute, I swapped some out for the gems. Bedazzled things up. A real

LEGO bandit would leave a fancier calling card than plain bricks."

I laugh. "Then what happened?"

Finn jams his stick in the dirt. End of run. "The usual. Pog pointed me out. They called security, who called the police, who called my parents, who were—furious? shocked?—that their son was apparently a bank robber this whole time."

I could relate, jewel thief that I am.

"Are they okay?"

He waves his arms around like the question doesn't matter. "They're fine. It's a new loop. But we're getting close. I can feel it."

So can I. "What next?"

16

FINN

Next I run the play again, but this time convince Ezra to abandon his lookout post and join the fray. His job? To distract Pog—tell him he needs help, tell him that his poor kitten is stuck in a tree, tell him anything.

It doesn't work. Pog checks the briefcase. I get caught again, worse this time around. My dad "does not recognize my own son." And my mom is apparently admitted to the hospital for the stress. I do feel kind of bad that time. But also it doesn't matter. Everything resets. No harm, no foul.

# 17 …

EZRA

Next I let Finn talk me into setting off the fire alarm as Mr. Pog checks the briefcase on his way out. I tell Finn it won't work. Tell him it'll just draw more attention. Tell him he's running out of good ideas.

We do it anyway. And it goes about as I expect.

★ 18 ★

FINN

Next: I cage the mice from classroom four and let them loose in the lobby. *Also no.*

19

EZRA

Puppies. Finn and I release *puppies* into the bank. Why, you ask? I'm convinced it's just because Finn wants to see puppies.

Does. Not. Work.

★ 20 ★

FINN

Chickens? *Still no. And gross.*

21

EZRA

"This isn't working," Finn says, pacing my front yard.

I fake-gasp. "Whatever gave you that idea?"

"I still think we can do this," he says, staring me down. "It's the right plan. We're close. But we need more."

I hate it when he gets that look in his eyes. Never good. "More what?"

"Ezra," Finn calls into my ear. "You in position? Repeat: You in position, Ezra? Over."

"You know we're not on walkie-talkies, right? These are my Bluetooth earbuds."

No response.

"You know we're not on walkie-talkies, right? *Over.*"

"Sure. But isn't this more fun? Over."

There's no time to answer. Because right then Shai, Dovi, and Menachem Mendel show up outside the bank. I do a double take. Rub my eyes.

"You came," I say. "I can't believe you came."

They all look at each other. "I mean," Shai starts, "this is very strange and mysterious."

"Texting us that there's some emergency," Menachem Mendel continues. "Asking us to come all the way here."

"My dad is not going to love it when he finds out I skipped school," Dovi adds. "But it's your bar mitzvah weekend. If you want to celebrate by meeting outside a bank in the city, who are we to argue?"

I stare at them, still barely able to believe that all I had to do to get them here was . . . ask. No tricks. No schemes. Just a quick text and—abracadabra—here they are. I think back to all the other loops. All those Fridays studying for school, my friends right there with me. All those unbearable Shabbos dinners, my friends suffering through the meal. All those Saturdays, all those Sundays. Always there.

Maybe Finn was right. Maybe I don't know what I have.

"Why are you wearing earbuds?" Dovi asks me.

I shrug him off. "Expecting an important call." This loop, they haven't met Finn and there's no time for introductions.

"We're not *robbing* the bank, are we?" Dovi jokes.

"Ha. Ha ha ha," I say. "You're so funny. When did you get so funny?"

"Dial it down," Finn says into my ears.

"Shhh," I snap, forgetting that they can't hear him.

Dovi's smile drops off his face. "*Are* you okay?"

"Pull it together," Finn tells me. "It's just another loop. Nothing matters, except what does."

It's a thought that my brain accepts and also doesn't.

"Two minutes," Finn says, which means that Mr. Pog got off the train at Herald Square. Finn's at the usual lookout point, up the unguarded fire escape above an "I Heart NYC Gifts" store. *My* usual lookout point. Today we've switched places. I'm on the ground and Finn's running ops.

"Listen," I say to my friends, trying to remember the explanation Finn and I landed on. Some complicated story about wanting to show them a family heirloom I was inheriting from my dead grandpa. But I feel so weird lying to them. (Which I know is extra weird, given how much I've lied to them already.) And I'm not sure I can pull off the excuse.

So I don't even try.

Instead, I lead them through the doors of the bank and point to a couch in the lobby, halfway between the tellers and the giant door to the main vault. "Would you guys mind waiting for me?"

Dovi: "No problem."

Shai: "For sure."

Menachem Mendel: "Whatever you need."

I'm stuck in a time loop, trying to rob a bank. And I have three friends who are here for me without question. I'm not sure which is more extraordinary.

I nod and begin the slow walk toward the teller line.

"And . . . we're a go," Finn says, announcing Mr. Pog's entry into the bank. The little bell above the door chimes its chime. "Taking up secondary position. Meet you at the rendezvous. Good luck."

"Thanks," I say. "You too."

Mr. Pog walks in, screaming into his jumbo-sized cell phone.

"And that's when I said there's no way we're releasing those receivables yet. Let them try to lawyer up."

He asks for the bank manager without ever pausing his call.

"And *he* said that the bonding company's ready to— Actually, hang on a sec." He snaps his fingers in the manager's face. "Can I get into my safety-deposit box?" Mr. Pog backs up again, speaks into his phone. "Anyway, so the bonding company goes . . ."

Even though he'll get it all back on the next loop, I don't feel great about stealing from Mr. Pog. But he's not the easiest guy to like.

He heads to the security guard—gives his ID and fingerprints and numeric code—and is led through the vault door to the rear of the bank. I wait the three seconds, find the assistant manager, and—

Totally freeze, forget the script.

"What's happening?!" Finn screams too loudly into my ears.

"You're the actor here," I mutter through gritted teeth. "Not me."

"Can I help you?" Charlotte Moyal asks.

"Grandpa Chandler is already in the vault!" Finn shouts, feeding me my line. "GRANDPA IS ALREADY IN THE VAULT!"

Ms. Moyal leans down, concern on her face. "Everything all right?"

"We're off course," Finn says. "Forget it. We'll run the loop again."

And *that* is enough to scare me into action.

"Grandpa Chandler is already in the vault?!" I start.

"Oh no! I'm late and sorry can I go back there I was supposed to meet him here fifteen minutes ago and he's going to be so mad at me if I don't catch up so we can look at my parents' wedding rings together because I'm an orphan and because they died and because because because—"

I even muster some tears.

"You forgot to sniffle," Finn says into my ear. He's out of breath, running along Thirty-Fourth Street to meet me outside the bank. "You forgot to sniffle!"

Sniffle.

Ms. Moyal's face softens. Got it.

"Oh, you poor dear," she says. "Of course. Yes, your grandfather already headed to the back. Right this way."

She leads me across the lobby and through the vault doors.

"Nice work," Finn says.

This is my first time back here, and I quickly orient myself to Finn's dirt map of the place. The vault is basically one long hallway. Halfway down, there are bathrooms on one side, doors leading to empty offices on the other. Between the offices is a small alcove with an out-of-service water fountain. And at the far end of the corridor, directly opposite the main vault door, is a small room lined with cabinets stretching up every wall. In the center of the room, Mr. Pog is leaning over a metal table transferring stacks of gold from a box into his briefcase. He's still on the phone.

"—whose secretary had the *nerve* to tell me—"

"I'll leave you here," Ms. Moyal says as we reach the midpoint of the hallway. She returns to the lobby and—like every loop—Mr. Pog doesn't look up, too busy, too focused.

I dart into the alcove, crouch down, wait.

"I'm here," I whisper to Finn.

"And I'm heading in," he says back as Mr. Pog returns the box to its sleeve in the wall, locks the cabinet, and clicks his briefcase closed. "He on the part about the secretary yet?"

"Yeah."

"Shoot. We're running out of time." Finn lowers his voice. "But I'm at the couch. Repeat: I'm at the couch."

I didn't need his narration. I can hear my other friends chatting around him.

Shai: "You've got to admit Ezra's been acting weird lately."

Menachem Mendel: "It's probably the bar mitzvah pressure. Remember when I nearly bolted from shul at mine?"

Shai: "You did *not*."

Menachem Mendel: "Did too. I had Parshat Naso. It was *a lot*."

Dovi: "I think this is something else. Ezra seems, I don't know, *extra* stressed. His whole fam does. It's been like this for a while. We need to do something."

Shai: "Yeah."

Menachem Mendel: "You're right."

Dovi: "We need to make sure he knows we're there for him."

Mr. Pog steps out of the safety-deposit room, his dress shoes clacking against the marble floor.

"Maybe we should call this off," I say, panic rising in my chest.

"What?!" Finn says. His voice is back to full volume. I can no longer hear Dovi, Shai, or Menachem Mendel. "No. Everything's in place."

"I don't want them to get hurt."

"They won't get hurt. They *can't* get hurt. No matter what happens, they won't remember it."

"Does that make enough of a difference?" I ask. Finn might be fine with all this, but I'm not.

"It's gonna be okay."

"Please. We can try another way."

"Do it!"

"No!"

"Yes!"

Mr. Pog is nearly on me now.

"Hold on," he says into his phone, speaking even louder than before. He pulls the phone from his ear as he walks, checking the screen. "It's Sean. I'll merge the calls."

That's the signal.

I can't think. There's not enough time. Finn's right and wrong. I can't stand the thought of my friends getting hurt. I can't stand the thought of having to do this all over again. And again. And again. My legs find a mind of their own. I rocket out of the alcove, crashing hard into Mr. Pog. His briefcase drops. I kick it backward, replacing it with the fake.

"Sorry," he says, picking up the decoy case, unbuttoning and rebuttoning his jacket. Someone's still talking from the speaker of his phone. Mr. Pog ends the call anyway. He extends a hand, helps me up. "Sorry, kid. Are you okay?"

Great. And now Mr. Pog is a real person too.

"Yeah, sorry, fine," I say as Mr. Pog continues toward the exit.

"No turning back now," Finn says into my ear.

And I follow the plan to the letter. The *new* plan.

Instead of walking out with the briefcase, I open

it up here and now—in the hallway, on the floor—and stuff the gold into a regular backpack I brought with me, ditching the empty case in one of the offices.

Then everything else happens all at once.

I return to the lobby. My friends stand and smile. Mr. Pog checks his briefcase near the exit and spills LEGO bricks all over the floor.

"Hey!" he shouts. "This isn't my briefcase. *WHERE'S MY BRIEFCASE?!*"

I catch Dovi move his head, notice something at his feet. He bends down, reaches beneath the couch, and pulls out *another* identical briefcase, the one Finn planted when he passed by. Shai does the same—another briefcase. Menachem Mendel, the same—another. Until all three of them are standing there, dazed, clutching briefcases they've never seen, as an angry man points at them, shouts at them, "Security! Security!"

They freeze, eyes wide.

"Ezra?" Dovi calls out.

"Ezra!" Finn whisper-shouts near the door. My other friends register the call. They turn toward Finn and see a kid they don't know. Then they turn to me and see a kid they thought they knew.

"Ezra, let's go!" Finn calls a little louder.

Three security guards appear from nowhere and

confront Dovi, Shai, and Menachem Mendel, surround them, box them in. One of my friends starts to cry, then another.

Mr. Pog marches forward, ignoring Finn, ignoring *me*. "Open the cases!" he shouts. "They—they took something from me!"

I'm steps from the exit now, unable to move. Finn grabs me by the arm, pulls me along. I allow myself to be dragged out of the bank, but not before making eye contact with a silent, shocked Dovi, his face all confusion and betrayal.

"Did you get it?" Finn asks as we step out onto the street.

From somewhere up the block, police sirens begin to scream. I loop my second arm through the loose backpack strap. "Yeah," I say, the gold heavy on my shoulders.

Finn breaks into a run.

I don't know what else to do other than follow him.

"It's only two days," Finn says, slapping me on the back. "They won't remember."

"I know," I say.

But I will.

★ 22 ★

FINN

I get it. I do. You don't want to frame your best friends for a crime they didn't commit. Totally reasonable. But time has already reset, so it's all good. And now we're that much closer to getting out of here.

Speaking of.

The Rosen family is right on time, just after three stars blink into existence in the night sky. I'm across the street, behind the tall bushes in the Milgroms' yard, watching the Rosens through their dining room window. They're running the Saturday night havdalah ritual that I've even attended a handful of loops. Like always, Ezra's dad lifts the full cup of wine. Like always, Eliana and Eitan argue over who gets to hold the braided candle.

Like always, Eliana wins, gripping the candle tight, dripping wax onto the paper plate in spiral patterns.

Mr. Rosen begins the end-of-Sabbath prayer—his mouth moves, a few seconds tick by—and then he puts down the cup, spilling a little wine as it touches the counter. He lifts the small spice container, shakes it a little, and smells the cloves inside. Mrs. Rosen takes a turn, then Avital, then all the kids on down. Next is the third blessing, which ends in hands tilted at the fire, little flames reflected in all their nails. And then Mr. Rosen lifts the cup a final time. He finishes havdalah and pours half the wine onto the plate. Eliana turns the candle upside down and extinguishes the flame.

It's been a few loops since the heist, and we've got a steady schedule. We're back to visiting Dr. London every Friday. We show her the gold-plated drive she made—containing her data and a video of herself explaining what's going on. Then we return to her office every Sunday, record a new video, and return the drive to Dr. London's desk.

In between, she's making progress. *Real* progress. And even if Ezra's mad at me, he knows we wouldn't be here if we hadn't pulled off the heist. But it's just as well.

I've got an errand to run, alone.

Havdalah ends, and the Rosen family scatters. The

parents to the kitchen. Esty and Eliana to play in the living room. Ezra and Eitan to their room. And Avital—

Avital runs upstairs for less than a minute before sneaking outside: through her bedroom window, across the roof, and down to her dad's car.

She starts the engine and pulls out of the driveway, headlights off to avoid attention. I knock the kickstand out from underneath my bike and follow her down the block. Because while Dr. London is making real progress, I haven't forgotten Plan A: the perfect loop. Finding problems, solving them. Ezra might be willing to rely on Dr. London. But I don't see why we can't loop and chew gum at the same time. And if Ezra won't do the hard work, I'll do it for him.

Down the dark residential street, left at the end. People are still walking home from Ezra's synagogue. I accidentally wave at Dovi Frisch, who's crossing the street with his dad, even though I haven't met either of them this loop around. Another left at the stop sign, onto the busier road that cuts Ezra's neighborhood in half. Avital speeds up, but there's enough stop-start traffic that I manage to keep her in my sights. Right at the light, over the train tracks. Past the new luxury apartments, still under construction. At first, I think she's driving to the Bergenville Hotel—over the bridge, down the main road. But instead, she slows in the little downtown of grocery stores and kosher restaurants.

The parking lot is already full. Avital loops around the block a few times, finds a space, gets out of the car. I ride past her, tilting my face away, irrationally afraid of being spotted by someone who's never seen me before. I lean my bike against a post and trail her the rest of the way on foot. She clutches her coat to her neck and passes two restaurants before ducking into a third: Naphtali's, that pizza place Ezra loves.

I follow her inside and toward the back.

I'm impressed at Ezra's solid instincts. Sneaking out to a restaurant on Saturday night? Afraid of being spotted by her parents? Self-conscious of whatever she's wearing? It all adds up to one thing—

"Gotcha!" I shout as she pops out of the bathroom. Her coat is off, replaced with a little paper cap and an apron, both of which read, "Bergenville's #1 Kosher Pizza." She's also wearing a long-sleeve T-shirt with little pizza toppings printed along the sides. Kind of an odd outfit for a date, but who am I to judge?

Avital doesn't flinch, assuming I'm not talking to her. "Can you move?"

"Where is he?" I ask.

She glances behind her, confirming that there's no

one else in this narrow hallway. "Where's *who*? Also—can you please move? I'm late."

A kid about Avital's age—a boy—comes into the restaurant and looks around, craning his neck. He decides to get on the line to order.

"Is that him?" I ask.

Avital's patience is spent. She crosses her arms. "Is that *who*?"

"Reuven Rothwax. Ezra told me you were dating him."

Avital barks out a laugh. "First, ew. Second, *ew*. Third, who are you?"

"He's not your secret boyfriend?"

Her mouth drops open. "My *what*?! Ezra thinks I have a secret boyfriend?"

So that *isn't* it. "Okay. You don't have a secret boyfriend. Then what's going on, Avital? Why are you sneaking out?" I wrote down a list of possibilities, once upon a loop. I try to recall which option I ranked number one. "Is this some, you know, rebellion against your community or something?"

She tilts her head. "Why would I rebel against my community? I *love* my community."

"Then what?"

She stares at me. Blinks for a few seconds. "You're a

friend of Ezra's?" she asks, stepping back, taking me in.

I nod.

She purses her lips, then calls behind her, toward the kitchen. "Tal, can I have an extra five minutes? I'll make it up at the end."

Someone grunts from near the pizza oven. "Sure thing."

Avital sighs and removes the hat from her head. She squeezes around me, leading us toward an open table in the main seating area of the restaurant. "Grab two sodas," she says, motioning toward the drink fridge. "On me."

We sit. I wait. She leans forward. "You sure know a lot about a lot for someone I've never met." She pauses. "You *think* you know a lot about a lot anyway."

"We've met," I say. "My parents pulled me out of Bnei Torah after second grade, but Ezra and I have stayed friends." I know from experience that this is the one quick line most likely to get Avital to accept my presence.

"If you say so," she says. "Now, about this whole Reuven Rothwax business."

"You're not dating him."

She shivers. "One thousand percent not."

"And you're not, I don't know, experiencing some crisis of faith."

She chuckles. "How old are you again? Why do you

even know the phrase 'crisis of faith'?"

"I am wise beyond my years," I answer.

"Clearly," she deadpans. "Listen, I'm going to tell you what's going on. I'm not sure I have a choice at this point. But I need you to promise me you won't tell Ezra. Not yet. *Please.*"

"Pinkie promise," I say, sticking out my littlest finger. But she doesn't take it, and I drop my hand.

"Thanks," she says, glancing down at the paper cap on the table, flattening out her apron. "Also, I feel like someone who's 'wise beyond their years' can crack this case. Isn't it obvious?"

Now that I'm taking a moment to think, it is. "You . . . work here."

She touches a finger to her nose. "Bingo."

"That doesn't seem so bad."

She smiles. "Gee, thanks! Honestly, the pay is abysmal, but at least there's free pizza."

"I don't get it though. Why sneak out?"

Avital takes a sip of her soda. "My dad. He doesn't want me to work. I mean, I'm going to seminary soon, then college. He knows I'm going to work *one day*. He wants me to focus on school right now, finals and all that, not worry about making money. But we *need* the money."

I wait, silently urging her on.

"You promise you won't tell Ezra," she says again.

I hold up my right hand, put the other on my heart. "In this timeline and every other."

She raises an eyebrow but continues. "Abba and Imma—they've been keeping it a secret. They want to wait until after the bar mitzvah. They don't want to spoil the weekend by telling him."

"Telling him *what*?"

She's not really looking at me, not really listening to me. "I guess that's why they didn't want me taking this job in particular. It's not like the Bergenville kosher pizza scene is that big. They were probably worried that one of Ezra's buddies would walk in, catch me here, and ask me what's going on." She fixes her eyes on me again. "A fair concern, apparently."

I wait a beat and then ask again: "Telling him *what*?"

"That . . . that we're moving. That they sold the house. The warehouse Abba works at closed, they cut his position. He's been interviewing for new jobs, and Imma's now doing private OT consultations on the side every afternoon. But it's not enough. I'm sure you've seen all those big houses going up on our block."

"The Milgroms," I say.

"And others. Taxes got too expensive. Everything got

too expensive. Food. Tuition. Camp. Shul. We can't keep up. So our parents sold the house to another family that's probably going to knock the whole thing down and we're leaving the neighborhood we've lived in forever. They found a place to rent in some cheaper town. Everything's going to change. And I thought... I thought I could help. They're not going to call off the move. I get that. But I'm eighteen. I want to chip in. Problem is, every time I bring up the idea, it makes Abba mad. So I took the job without telling him. And it feels good, to be a little self-sufficient. I am not going to let him talk me out of it."

She wipes her eyes. "I don't know why I'm telling you all this. I still don't ever remember meeting you, but then maybe..." She shakes her head. "I guess it's nice to get things off my chest."

"Wow," I say. "Ezra's going to be—well, I'm not sure what he's going to be. Surprised, for one thing."

She points a finger at me. "You're not going to tell him. Not before this weekend is up. You promised."

"I did. But all this time. I can't believe Ezra hasn't put the pieces together himself."

There's a sudden shout from the kitchen. "Avital! We could use your help back here! Motzei Shabbos rush!" The line behind the counter is getting longer, stretching toward increasingly full tables.

"Coming!" Avital shouts, standing up. She looks down at me before leaving, returning the paper cap to her head. "As for Ezra not putting the pieces together? We see what we want to see, I guess."

"But right under his nose?"

Avital takes a step backward. "Sometimes that's the stuff we have the most trouble seeing."

✶ 23 ✶

EZRA

Loop after loop after loop.

But it doesn't feel as bad as it used to, or as pointless. It's the same, and it's not the same at all. We've got a goal. An end in sight. Dr. London melted the gold down, used it to cover the little drive in a kind of metal net. I don't understand how the thing works, but it does. And now she can save her work from one loop to the next.

"Be back in a few," I tell my family, looking up at the clock. It's Sunday. Almost time for our meeting with Dr. London on the far side of the hotel. My mom is absentmindedly fixing balloons to the tables. My dad is angrily unstacking chairs in a corner. Avital is setting up the music, Esty on her hip. And Eitan's pretending to watch

Eliana while watching sports highlights on his phone instead. No one so much as glances in my direction as I leave Ballroom C.

Finn's bar mitzvah party begins earlier than mine and dries up before I start my speech. My end of the hallway is relatively quiet, but music is already blaring from inside Ballroom A, and some people are beginning to arrive. Finn's parents stand together on one side of the ballroom doors, hand in hand, welcoming people in.

"Finn?" I call out into the empty Ballroom B. Our usual meeting spot. The lights are off, the room is still. Through the false wall on my left, I can hear a few kids chatting inside Finn's party:

"Why did we come to this?"

"My mom said I only have to be here for an hour."

"Yeah, no way I'm staying longer than that."

Through the wall on my right, my dad and Avital are starting round one:

"I don't want to talk about this now, Abba."

"You don't want to talk to me *ever*. Please. I just need to know where you were last night."

"No," she says. "You don't."

"Ask Reuven Rothwax," I say out loud to the empty Ballroom B. And then—

"Yo." Finn pops up from behind me, startling me a little. "Ready?"

"Sure."

We head down the hallway, through the lobby, toward the main conference center. We've got a good thing going with Dr. London, but Finn and I—we've lost a bit of our rhythm since the big heist. (If we ever had any rhythm, I guess.) We're not fighting, exactly. It's more the opposite. It's all a little quieter than it used to be. I'm still upset about getting my friends in trouble. He's still upset that I'm upset, wanting me to be perfectly fine, wanting me to, like, thank him for one of the worst days of my life or something. I'm waiting for an apology from him. He's waiting for an apology from me. And in the meantime:

"How many loops has it been since the heist?" I ask, making conversation. "Ten?"

"Eleven," Finn corrects, not looking at me.

"Eleven." I whistle. "Dr. London must be almost done by now, right?"

"It'll take however long it takes," he says.

End of chat.

We enter the walkway connecting the two halves of the hotel. Finn loops his student pass around his neck. I do the same. We head to the conference exhibit hall, and the registrar lets us pass without question. The room is mostly empty. It'll soon be dismantled, reset for the final keynote speeches. Finn leads us the long way around so we can stop at the "Six Flavours" concession stand. Finn orders a "lepton lemonade" for himself, and a "subatomic deli sub" for Dr. London.

But something's wrong.

"How'd you know?" Dr. London usually asks when we get to her office and Finn holds out her favorite sandwich. Then she usually catches herself. "Right. Of course. Thanks."

This time, she looks up at us, her face pale. "I'm not hungry."

Finn and I glance at each other. It's a new version of the Sunday meeting, and not one we want.

"What happened?" Finn asks, sitting in one of two chairs opposite Dr. London. I join him in the other.

"I . . . ," she starts. "You're stuck in a time loop, and I'm helping you."

Finn leans forward. "We covered this on Friday. We cover this every Friday."

"I know, I know. I watched the video. I reviewed the data. I believe you. I believe *me*. I'm helping you."

She's not making sense.

"Then what's the problem?" I ask, the look on her

face sending a bolt of terror through my body. My whole life flashes before my eyes—but it's only three days long, and also infinite. A life where I never get older. A life where I relive my bar mitzvah and relive my bar mitzvah and relive my bar mitzvah, never ending. Never.

Dr. London turns her computer around, showing us a familiar Excel spreadsheet. It's overflowing with numbers and symbols neither one of us understands.

"*That's* the problem!" She slaps the table and stands. "I was running a few simulations yesterday and kept getting the same error. At first, I thought it was me. That I'd made a mistake. Missed something. I mean, I'm communicating with iterative versions of myself. There are bound to be complications. But the model is sound, and it retains at least *some* basic modification metadata from one loop to the next."

Finn grips the sides of his chair. "And?"

Dr. London leans over us and points to a few rows of data displayed on her screen. "And that's it right there," she says, clicking a button, turning a third of the numbers blinking red. "The smoking gun. All the evidence you need."

"Evidence of *what*?" I ask.

She steps toward the door and stops. "I think . . . ," she answers, speaking to the wall, her back to us, her voice barely above a whisper. "I think the data has been *altered*."

"Altered?" I repeat.

She turns around. "It's all wrong. There are missing cells. Raw numbers where there should be formulas. Formulas that may as well be gibberish. I'm *positive* the changes weren't there on Friday. . . ." Dr. London trails off.

"What are you saying?" Finn asks, standing to join her. She scans his face, as much terror in it as I feel.

"I think you know what I'm saying."

"Can you fix it?" Finn asks.

Dr. London returns to her computer and begins typing. "Yes. But it's a significant setback. I'm not at square one, however. . . ."

"Bad data can be worse than none at all," I say.

The room goes quiet.

A significant setback.

All those loops for nothing.

"What does it all mean?" I ask, to Dr. London, to Finn, to myself. "What's happening? How was the data altered?"

Finn looks down at me, his eyes wide. "There's only one explanation," he says. "I can't believe I haven't considered it before."

"Considered *what*?"

"I was so focused on making contact with you—and then we were both so focused on breaking out together—that we forgot to ask one crucial question."

"Which is?"

"Think about it," Finn continues. "How many things have gone wrong? All those failed bar mitzvah loops. The lottery. The bank robbery."

Dr. London's head snaps toward us. "You robbed a bank?"

Finn ignores her. "Why isn't this *easier*? Why do we keep *losing*? All this time—you're here, I'm here. But what are the odds? Why would we be the only ones? Why would we ever think we were alone?"

I understand and I don't. "What does it *mean*?" I ask again.

"What if," Finn says, his face pale, sunken, "there's someone else out there, someone who also *remembers* from loop to loop. What if they've been out there the whole time. And what if . . . they're trying to stop us."

★ 24 ★

FINN

"Why would anyone try to stop us?" Ezra asks me the next Loop-Friday morning. "Why would anyone want us to be stuck like this?"

We're circling the Bergenville hallways, having finished getting Dr. London up to speed, again. We explained the new development. And she's still willing to help us. But new Dr. London has the same take as the last version:

The data has been altered.

It's all wrong.

A significant setback.

Just thinking the words twists me up inside.

"No clue," I say, sorting through potential explanations in my mind, wishing so badly that I could give him answers. "Maybe one of us has a secret archenemy who is bent on keeping us here at all costs. Maybe one of us will eventually become a hero who saves the world in the future—and the bad guys went back in time, trapped us here, and don't want to let us out. Oh." I freeze for a moment, look over at Ezra. "Maybe *we* become the villains—and it's the good guys who trapped us here."

Ezra takes a few seconds to mull it all over. "I guess none of that's weirder than what's happened so far," he says. "The *why* of it isn't the most important question right now anyway."

"What do you mean?"

"Well, whoever's out there knows about us, right? About the time loop. About what we're doing to escape. They know about Dr. London and the drive, and they sabotaged us."

"I'm with you so far," I say.

Ezra rubs his eyes. It's still morning. We always wake up on Friday rested and refreshed. He's exhausted anyway. We both are. "What makes us think this person won't . . . strike again?" he asks. "Mess with the drive when Dr. London isn't looking. Then we'll be right back here, *again*. And again. And again."

I nod, Ezra's words hitting me like a punch in the gut. "What are you suggesting? That we give up? Stop trying to get out?"

Now it's Ezra's turn to freeze. "No way. Is that what *you* think we should do?"

I jut out my jaw. "Absolutely not. I think . . ." A light bulb goes off in my head. It's not going to be easy. We'll need to plan, set everything up. But it might be the only way. "I think we need to lay ourselves a trap."

Ezra smiles. "Exactly."

"I am so excited!" Ezra shouts at me the next Loop-Friday around. We're wandering every inch of the hotel, Ezra showing off his awful acting skills to anyone in earshot. People in the lobby. Hotel employees. Anyone. Everyone. We've got to get the message out far and wide. Cheese on the mousetrap. "We sure will be out of this time loop soon! Yep! Any day now!"

"You know it!" I say. People are staring. Good. Let them. "Dr. London says she's never been closer! Antidote, here we come. And *all* the data she needs is right on that drive!"

"Right on that drive, you say?" Ezra yells.

"YES! RIGHT ON THE DRIVE!"

★ ★ ★

To Ezra's family and friends, that night at dinner: "And that's when we realized that someone was messing with us."

I'm just going for it, sitting around the table, telling the entire story. I fork a giant cube of potato kugel, holding it up like a candied apple.

"Thankfully," I add, "Dr. London already managed to fix everything." That part isn't true. Not yet. "Now we sit back and wait. As long as nothing happens to the drive, this might be the last run. We are *really* close to the end."

Ezra's dad takes a sip of water. Ezra's mom gives me a polite smile and serves herself a bit more olive dip. "You didn't tell us your new friend has such a . . . vivid imagination, Ezra."

"Tell everyone you know!" Ezra says.

At Ezra's synagogue the next morning:

"Ya'amod!" the gabbai calls out, using the words that announce it's Ezra's turn to make his main blessing at the Torah. "Ha'bochur ha'bar mitzvah, Ezra Akiva ben Yosef Yerachmiel, maftir!"

Ezra rolls the two arms of the Torah shut, hands clasping the wooden handles. But this time, before making the blessing, he looks up:

"Quick dvar Torah!" he calls to the crowded synagogue. A confused murmur spreads out from the center of the room.

"Um, Ezra," Rabbi Neumann says from his seat, "why don't we save speeches for later? Maybe the kiddush? Let's get straight to maftir and the haftorah."

Ezra nods. "Oh, sure, Rabbi." Then he waits a few seconds and tells the entire congregation that we're two kids trapped in a time loop and that tomorrow's probably the last chance for someone to stop us from getting out.

Crickets around the room. Ezra's dad slumps down. His mom and Avital look at each other like they've accidentally landed on another planet. Mr. Bendish *gets up and storms out.*

"Tough crowd," I mutter.

Ezra concludes, "Amen."

This is the plan. Getting the word out to as many people as possible. If there's someone out there trying to stop us, they'll think they need to try again. Now.

"And this time," I tell Ezra, "we'll be ready."

It's Loop-Sunday again. We're back at the Bergenville, in Dr. London's office. We switched out the real Faraday drive for a fake and, while Dr. London is off doing her work in the hotel café, Ezra and I are here, waiting.

"Do you think someone will show?" Ezra whispers to me after a while. We're crouched behind Dr. London's desk, watching the door for signs of life. The fake drive is sitting on the desk, bait at the end of a fishing hook.

"No idea. But if they've really been watching us, how could they not?"

Ezra growls. "I am so angry. I can't believe anyone would do this. Torture us like this. Keep us trapped. It's so *wrong*."

"We're just kids," I agree.

"And we're going to stay that way forever if this doesn't work," Ezra says. "Ugh."

Ugh is right. I'm as angry as Ezra. It is so unfair. *Life* is so unfair. I try to put how I'm feeling into words that will make sense. But before I get the chance, footsteps materialize on the other side of the door.

My heart pounds.

The doorknob turns.

Someone walks inside, toward the desk.

Ezra's eyes go wide. His hands are shaking. We've gone over this. We'll stay hidden, ID the perp, let him take the drive. We've equipped this fake with GPS tracking and should be able to follow it, at least until the loop resets. We'll gather clues, learn as much as we can, for however long it takes to solve this new mystery.

But—

"I can't do this," Ezra says, his fists clenched.

Before I can stop him, just as the stranger plucks the decoy drive off the table, Ezra shoots up from our hiding spot.

"Aha!" he shouts. "We caught you!"

I stand, try to pull Ezra back. But he's too upset. He's feet shorter than the stranger but gets in his face anyway, a finger at his face. "How *could* you?!"

The man is—

Familiar. Tall. Name tag: "Andy Pauli."

"You . . . You're . . . ," Ezra stutters, trying to make sense of what he's seeing. "You work at the front desk."

"Only on Tuesdays and Saturdays," Andy says, the usual sneer on his face. "Otherwise I'm *concierge at large*."

Ezra shakes his head to clear it. "Now that I think about it, it's so obvious. You were there—that first day Finn and I met. *Really* met. You were there—the first time we tried to get into the conference. You're always there, slowing us down, getting in our way." Ezra's hands are grabbing at his hair like he might yank it out. "Concierge at large. Whatever that means. We *caught* you." He points to the drive. "Why? Why are you doing this?"

The man opens his palm, revealing the drive. "It's my

job," he says, blinking, clocking me and Ezra, alone in this dark office. "I should ask what *you* are doing here."

"Argh!" Ezra screams, furious at the non-answers. He looks back at me. He needs help. This wasn't the plan, but plans change. I get in the man's face too. "Tell us who you work for."

Ezra joins in. "Yeah! Who do you work for?!"

"Who do you work for?!"

"Who do you work for?!"

And suddenly this guy is against the wall, visibly disturbed at being screamed at by two thirteen-year-old kids.

"Tell us!"

"WHO. DO. YOU. WORK. FOR?!"

"Bergenville Hotels LLC!" he answers, tapping the little logo on his name tag, eyes flinching shut. "Bergenville Hotels LLC!"

"The hotel," Ezra breathes. "Of course."

I whistle. "It must go straight to the top."

"This place," Ezra says, spinning in a circle, hands back on his head. "They're messing with us. I bet this is all some horrible experiment. They have security cameras everywhere, Finn. *Everywhere*. They've been watching us this whole time. I feel sick."

Ezra shrieks, grabs the fake drive from the concierge's

palm. He chucks it to the floor, crushes it beneath his shoe. Andy shimmies his way along the office wall toward the still-open door.

"I . . . I'm calling security. Yes, that's it. Stay here. I'm calling security."

Andy runs down the hall. I move to follow.

"We need to track him," I say, improvising.

Ezra moves in the opposite direction. "We need to tell Dr. London what's happening. This whole place is a trap. She could be in danger."

I run alongside Ezra, through the conference space hallways, across the lobby, up the steps to the café.

"She could be *in* on it," I warn Ezra, my brain reeling with the possibilities. He nearly trips on the stairs at this news. I catch him before he falls. We continue the rest of the way.

The café is relatively empty. A few familiar faces from the physics conference. A kid coloring in a notebook while their dad orders two hot chocolates from the counter. And Dr. London, sitting there. Unmoving.

Her hands are set in her lap, her eyes locked on her computer screen.

"Hey, Doc?" I try.

At first she doesn't respond.

"Dr. London?" Ezra tries, waving a hand in front of

her eyes. "Everything okay?"

She takes a deep breath—waits: one, two—before finally exhaling and looking up at us. She reaches to turn the computer around. It's her data again. I never completely understand what I'm seeing, but I understand enough. The red marks are back, infecting the entire screen.

"It happened again," she says. "We've been so careful. At least, I think we have. But it happened again. And this time, it's everything."

Ezra stumbles, collapses into a chair. I just stand there, watching the scene play out. It's like I'm not even really here, it's like something out of a bad dream.

"My work," Dr. London says. "All my work. It's gone."

25

EZRA

I move through time like a ghost. Wake up. Friday morning with Dr. London. School with my friends. Shabbos dinner with my family. Reading from the Torah. Sunday morning with Dr. London. Party—

Wake up. Friday morning. School. Shabbos. Torah. Sunday morning. Party—

Wake up. Friday. Shabbos. Sunday. Party—

Friday. Shabbos. Sunday.

Friday. Shabbos. Sunday.

Friday. Shabbos. Sunday.

I'm barely here, floating from one moment to the next. Nothing sticks in my memory. In one ear, out the other. It all blurs together.

Finn tells me not to worry. That Dr. London will finish her work this time. And if not this time, next time. If not next time, the time after that.

We keep searching for whoever is doing this to us. Every road is a dead end.

We've confronted Andy Pauli three loops in a row. He always acts the same: "No running in the hotel!" "No yelling in the hotel!" He doesn't seem to like us very much, but he also doesn't seem to dislike us enough to trap us in a time loop. He always pretends to know nothing: "Which drive?" "Doctor *what now*?" "I'm sorry, a *time loop*? Can you please leave me alone? I have real work to attend to." And you can always predict where he's going to be: Wandering near the hotel entrance on Friday. Behind the desk on Saturday. Policing the conference on Sunday. Again and again and again. Other than the one time we caught him in Dr. London's office, he's never done anything out of the ordinary, never left the track he's on from the beginning of the loop to the end.

Finn thinks he's telling the truth, that he doesn't know anything, that he's a pawn in some bigger game. But if this really does go all the way to the top, we can't seem to climb very far. The hotel manager doesn't work weekends, and his house is dark from Friday to Sunday (and alarmed, as one unfortunate loop made very clear).

The regional vice president is based out of a Bergenville Hotel in Rahway, but she's out on medical leave for the next month. And the CEO of the company is away at a corporate retreat in Colorado.

Last few loops: We changed tactics. Buddied up to Frank, the chief hotel security guard. With the right coffee (cappuccino, three sugars, extra hot) delivered at the right time (1:58 p.m. Friday), he'll let us watch the public-area camera feeds from his office. But no one ever does anything suspicious. Another dead end.

No one knows anything.

No one can do anything.

It's all pointless.

Dr. London announces to me and Finn that she's back on track, that her work is almost complete, that she's nearly ready to make the antidote—as long as no one deletes her data. But I know it's only a matter of time.

"What's the next move?" Finn asks. It's Friday again. "I was thinking of heading to the county courthouse. They might have government records on who owns the land the Bergenville was built on. Could be another angle."

"No," I say as we step out of the lobby. Some loops I bike to school with Finn. Today, I want to walk alone.

"Come on," Finn insists, jogging to keep up with me. "We can't give up. Not when we're so close."

His words feel like a slap in the face. I stop and spin around. "*So close?* How many times have we been *so close*? Can we even count?"

"This is different."

"*How? How is this different?* How is anything ever different?"

"Dr. London—"

"Dr. London can't help us, don't you get it? No matter what we do, something is going to go wrong. Her work will be ruined. Again. And then we'll have to start over. Again. I can't do it anymore. It feels like . . . it feels like I'm trapped in a room and all I want to do is get to the other side. But when I open the door . . . there's just another door. And then another. And another. How many times am I supposed to turn the knob before I give up, huh? A hundred? A thousand? I can't do it anymore, Finn. I can't keep getting my hopes up. It's too much. It's too hard. There's nothing we can do to keep the drive—"

Something sparks in my mind. I go silent for a moment, feeling alive for the first time in a long time. Could it really be that simple?

Finn waves a hand in front of my face. "Earth to Ezra! Hello!"

I blink. "I figured it out."

"Figured *what* out?"

"We don't know who's messing with us. They're too clever. Fine. Maybe that's the wrong approach. Maybe we stop trying to figure out who's behind the sabotage and focus on the drive itself. Protecting it."

I turn around, start back to the hotel.

Finn smiles huge and follows. "Okay! Now we're talking. What do you have in mind? Where do we start?"

"Your plans are too complicated," I say. "Making a fake drive and setting it out as bait? Trying to convince the CEO's secretary that we're his long-lost twin sons?"

"Hey, she didn't hang up on us that time."

"She didn't hang up on us *right away*," I correct. "We need to think simpler. If we want to protect the drive, let's protect the drive. Keep it safe!" I laugh to myself.

"Meaning..."

"Meaning, let's buy a safe and lock the thing inside while Dr. London isn't using it."

Finn shakes his head. "I've considered that. It doesn't work. The drive has to be kept in the desk drawer from one loop to the next, remember? There's no room for a safe in there."

I rack my brain. "Okay. Okay. So we make the whole office a safe. We leave the drive where it is and... replace her office door. Install new locks. State of the art. We bank-vault the thing."

"Now who's thinking too complicated? How are we supposed to replace Dr. London's door in a single loop?"

I stop again. "We won the lottery!" I shout.

Andy Pauli's outside by the hotel parking lot. He barks at us to stop yelling. I roll my eyes and lower my voice.

"We won the lottery. We robbed a bank. You were once elected mayor of your town." A loop that went a little off the rails. Don't ask. "You don't think we can convince Frank to replace a *door*?"

Finn sighs. "I don't know . . ."

"Please," I say. "What can it hurt. Let's see a plan of *mine* through for once."

And we put things into motion.

One loop: We ask Frank for help directly, bring him a cappuccino every day. It doesn't work.

Another: We break down the door, stage a fake robbery, try to convince Frank that the office isn't secure enough. But he just calls the police and puts a little orange cone where the door used to be.

And another: Dr. London calls Frank directly and requests a better lock, "to protect my very important work." But instead of changing the door, the front desk loans her a fancier office on the fourth floor of the hotel.

Trial and error, as Finn says. What finally does the trick is a call to security from the hotel manager—or, at least, Finn pretending to be the manager, using a voice-modulation app that he downloads for five bucks. We ask Frank about his kids, recommend a few museums for the vacation he's taking next month, and then hit him with instructions to upgrade the door on orders of the CEO himself.

"ASAP," Finn says over the phone. "And I'm talking *ASAP*. Spare no expense. I want Fort Knox, Frank, do you hear me? Fort. Knox."

Triple locks. Retina scans. Thumbprints. Only me, Finn, and Dr. London allowed.

"Let's see them get through that," I say.

Finn smiles and raises his hand for a high five. "Never gonna happen," he agrees as we slap palms and each go home for the weekend, Dr. London locked in her office, the drive secure.

Friday night dinner goes like always. I just want to push past it, get to the other side. I don't even bother following my mom to the garage. I wake up on Shabbos morning itching to call Dr. London, but I can't use the phone until sundown. I consider walking to the hotel after Torah reading, which I rush through on triple speed, but Mr. Bendish talks at me for like an hour when shul is done, more worked up than ever about all my many leining mistakes.

When Saturday night comes, my dad can't say havdalah fast enough. I pass around the besamim so quick that half the container spills out onto the floor.

"Let's go, let's go," I say, waving my hands at the candle, nearly blowing it out.

And the moment the fire is properly extinguished, I bolt out of the room, beat everyone upstairs. Grab my phone, turn it on, ring Dr. London.

"Pick up," I say to myself. "Please."

It's been a whole day. Anything can happen in a whole day.

"This is Dr.—"

"Dr. London. This is Ezra. You know, one of the kids trapped in the time loop."

Dr. London chuckles. "Hard to forget you, Ezra." She pauses. "Except every time I do, I guess. How can I help you? I thought we usually speak again on Sunday morning."

"We do, we do. I wanted to make sure everything is okay. That your data is still there."

I hear a few clacks of her keyboard. "I'm in the office

now, actually. About to head out for dinner. Everything's here. All is fine. I'll make sure to lock up this fortress of yours on my way out."

I breathe a sigh of relief. "Okay. Thanks. And yeah, see you tomorrow."

"See you tomorrow."

Click.

I text Finn. Let him know I checked in. That we're so far, so good. He thumbs-up reacts and sends me three muscle-arm emojis in response.

Except—

Sunday morning is forever from now. I hear Avital run to her room. Eitan follows her upstairs, changing into shorts and a T-shirt to shoot baskets across the street at the Milgroms' hoop. I grab a book from the floor—something I've read a hundred times. I open it up, can't take in a single word. I keep rereading the same sentence over and over. Outside, the car turns on. Avital pulls out of the driveway, making her usual escape to who-knows-where. I can't focus. Sunday morning. It's so far away.

I have to check.

It can't hurt to check, right?

I have to check.

I hop off my bed, throwing the book across the room. It hits Eitan in the shoulder as he's lacing up his sneakers.

"Hey!" he shouts. "What's your problem?"

"Sorry!" I dash out of the room, thunder down the stairs, throw the door wide open.

"Avital?" my dad calls from somewhere, mistaking my loud exit for something else.

But Avital's already gone. And I'm not her.

I slam the door behind me, hop on my bike.

Past shul. Over the tracks. Through downtown, where I can smell Naphtali's Pizza getting ready for the Motzei Shabbos crowd. I'm riding as fast as I can, wheels turning, wheels turning. Pumping my legs feels good. I know I'm worrying over nothing. It's been more than a dozen loops since the thief messed with us. Maybe he's gone. Maybe he's given up trying to get the drive.

Or maybe he was waiting until we gave him a sign that the drive was worth getting.

I ditch my bike in the middle of the parking lot and sprint into the hotel. Through the lobby—Andy shouts at me to stop running—down the hall. Across the walkway and into the meeting center.

It's late. There are no voices. No meetings in any of the rooms near Dr. London's office. The conference dinner is happening in the hotel restaurant at this exact moment. I should be all alone.

I take a beat, out of breath, hands on my knees. I look up at the intensely secured door in front of me, place my ear against it. All quiet. I laugh to myself. No one's in there. No one's getting through those locks. Another thought occurs to me—maybe we have this all wrong. Maybe Dr. London made some mistakes. Nobody's perfect. Sometimes getting things right takes a few turns around. Maybe there's no secret villain. No thief. No one out to get us.

But I came all this way. May as well check.

I press my finger to the first lock. A small screen flashes blue, followed by a message asking me to lean in close so it can scan my eye. I get through that step and the next, inputting the password we programmed yesterday: "FINN AND EZRA'S BAR MITZVAH TIME L00P"—with zeroes instead of O's.

The final bolt on the door slides open, and I pull the handle toward me.

It's dark inside, like it should be. It takes my eyes a split second to adjust from the bright hallway. The room is as we left it. The chairs. The desk. And to the side—

My heart thrums in my chest.

My whole body begins to shake.

My legs tense, wanting to run.

There's someone else here. Short, near the desk. The figure is faced away from me, hair hidden by the hood of a sweatshirt draped over their head. A head that's tilted down. I follow the gaze to the figure's extended hand, the Faraday drive resting in their open palm.

"Stop," I say. The word comes out hoarse, uncertain, broken. I take a deep breath. It's up to me now. There's no time to find Dr. London, no time to call Finn. I consider screaming. I still want to run. But I can't let them get away with this.

"Stop," I say again.

The figure closes a hand against the drive.

"Why are you doing this?" I ask. "We just want to leave." Tears sting my eyes. "We just want to grow up."

"But we can't," the figure says.

And if *seeing* him terrified me, *hearing* him feels like the ground opens beneath my feet. The world goes dark and cold.

I know that voice.

The figure turns around.

I know this kid.

Jeans and a hoodie. Glasses. A kind-of shoulder slouch that makes him look like he's leaning in close to hear what you've got to say.

I lift a hand to steady myself on the door frame. The room spins. My stomach ties in knots. I don't understand. I don't understand *anything*.

The kid lowers his hoodie.

"Hey, Ezra," Finn says.

26

FINN

"You?" Ezra says. It's not really a question.

I walk forward, one hand gripped on the drive, the other up—palm raised and open. I can't believe I've been this careless. I should have waited longer. Come here in the middle of the night. Or maybe tricked Dr. London into switching drives with me again. But when Ezra texted me *so far so good*, I thought he was off the trail for a bit.

I thought wrong.

He recoils, tripping backward through the office door. I step again. He stumbles across the hallway. Another step—and he slams against the opposite wall like I'm some monster.

And maybe I am.

"Let me explain," I say, even though I know it's too late for explanations, too late to turn back the clock.

"Was it you from the start?"

I open my mouth to answer, but Ezra speaks again before I get the chance. "Every time something went wrong—it was *you*, wasn't it? You told me there was a villain out there. And it was you."

I shake my head. "No, Ezra, listen—"

Ezra clenches his eyes shut—"*You* put me here"—and opens them again wide, terrified, panicking like a caged animal. He scans both ends of the empty hallway like maybe I'm not the only monster, like maybe they're around every corner. He looks back at me. "All this is because of you?"

"Ezra, calm down, please, listen—"

"That first loop. When we met. You'd been following me around. You were already the big expert in time loops. I can't believe I didn't see what was happening from the start. *You* did this to me. You did all of this."

"That's not true," I say. "You *know* it's not true. How could I? It doesn't make any sense."

"Finn, it's the only thing that makes sense. Of *course* you did this."

"I didn't!" A knot tightens in my chest. I can feel

myself getting upset. I was going to tell Ezra eventually. Tell him everything. Maybe in another loop. Maybe in ten. I'd pictured that moment in my mind. Practiced what I would say, how I would begin.

It's going all wrong. "You're not listening!" I shout.

Ezra laughs, half at me, half at himself. "A decoy drive! Your idea to catch the thief—your *fake* idea—was basically the same plan as the briefcases from the bank! And I *still* didn't see it! What was Andy even doing there that night?"

"Nothing really," I say. No reason for secrets now. "I emailed in a lost-and-found claim. Pretended to be a guest who left something behind in the office."

"Unbelievable. And I was supposed to, what, let Andy take the drive while we followed the GPS around town?"

Actually, I was going to steal it back and ship it to Canada, really confuse things. But that detail doesn't seem relevant at the moment.

"The drive was me," I confess. "I've been messing with Dr. London's data. Yes. But *nothing* else. Nothing. Else. I was trying to escape, same as you. Until—"

"Until *what*?!" he snaps.

My voice catches in my throat. I want to tell Ezra. But not like this. I can't talk about it like this.

He confuses my silence for another confession. "That's what I thought. I don't know *how* you trapped me here, Finn, but I do know *why*."

My heart flutters. *He knows?* And he never told me?

"I've seen the turnout at your bar mitzvah party," he says. "I've heard your so-called friends talking. Not exactly the most popular kid in school, are you?"

I've had one fist closed around the drive this whole time. Now I tighten the other. "What is *that* supposed to mean?"

"All those loops at my school. All that time with my friends. All those Friday nights and Shabbos days with my family. It was all some game to you, wasn't it? We *hurt* people. I know they reset on the next loop. But I still have nightmares. My parents at the jewelry store. My friends at the bank. Even Mr. Pog. And for what?"

I want to explain. But he won't let me get a word in edgewise.

"Just to avoid being alone, right?" Ezra says. "Just to keep me trapped here as your little pet. You were, what, jealous? No wonder we spent all those loops in my timeline instead of yours. That night at your house. You told me that I didn't know what I had. But *you* knew, didn't you? Because you *don't* have it."

I still feel guilty for what I've done to Ezra. I do. But his words send that piece of me tumbling somewhere deep down inside my brain. "Oh, don't flatter yourself. I wouldn't stay stuck in here another minute with you if I had a choice."

"Liar!" Ezra seethes. "I see everything perfectly clear now."

"You don't see *anything*. You should be thanking me for sabotaging the drive. You're not ready for what's on the other side."

The anger in Ezra's face cracks for a moment. "What are you talking about?"

"*Everything*," I answer, getting in his face. "I'm talking about everything. Avital doesn't have a secret boyfriend. She has a secret *job*. Your family is broke. They sold your house. They're just waiting until after the bar mitzvah to tell you that your *whole life* is about to change."

"How do you know that?"

"How do you not?! Like you said, I've spent most of the last hundred loops *away* from my family. What's your excuse?"

His nostrils flare. The anger returns. "You can't stop lying," Ezra says, throwing up his hands. "I'm done."

He turns to march down the hall. Half of me wants

to shoot off in the opposite direction. The other half wants to follow, make him understand, loop this conversation again and again until it goes the way I want.

"Stay away from me," Ezra says, his back still turned. "You want to be stuck in here so bad, *fine*. Do it alone."

27

EZRA

I swing the fridge doors open the moment I get home, tearing into the leftover food from shul lunch. It takes me two pieces of schnitzel and like four sprinkle cookies (and then two more) before I cool down.

Finn. This whole time, it was Finn.

Was I too mean? Can you be *too mean* to a kid who trapped you in a time loop? Yeah, I heard him. I know Finn said it *wasn't* him. That he only started messing things up *lately*. But Finn is also a liar.

"Hey," Eitan says. He bounds into the kitchen, sweating from his workout, basketball under his arm. I slide the tray of schnitzel across the counter. He stabs a cutlet with a plastic fork and starts nibbling at the edges. "There any bread?"

I nod at the package of half-eaten challah rolls. Eitan's always ravenous on Saturday night.

"Sweet," he says, moving to wash his hands with the cup on the counter—once, twice, three times, repeat.

I glance at the clock on the wall. If Eitan's back for his post-Shabbos melaveh malkah snacking, it means Avital's about to—

"I can't believe she did it anyway," my dad says from upstairs, opening the door to his room as a car pulls into the driveway.

"Let her be," my mom calls after him. "There are worse things."

"There are *better* things," my dad says.

They walk down the steps. Avital tries to sneak in quiet—key slid slowly into the lock, door pulled gentle so it doesn't creak. But they're already waiting for her, my mom leaning against the stairs, my dad with his arms crossed.

"Hi, Abba," Avital says all casual. She slips off her shoes, hangs her coat on the rack. The whole house smells like pizza from—

"Where have you been?" my dad asks. I mouth

along to the words. They've had this argument endless times.

Avital: "I went out."

Abba: "I can't have you doing this."

Avital: "I'm eighteen. I can do what I want."

Abba, angry: "You live in *this* house."

Avital, sarcastic: "Not for long."

Eitan steps into the living room, a challah roll in each hand. "What's going on?" he asks. I'm standing behind him, watching the scene play out.

Here's how it usually goes:

My dad turns to Eitan. "This doesn't concern you."

"Yosef," my mom scolds at his tone.

Then Avital takes advantage in the break from my parents' attention. She slides past them, heads up the stairs. "Sorry," she usually calls down to me. "Hope you're enjoying your bar mitzvah."

Next: Avital escapes to her room, locks the door.

Next: My dad follows, bangs a few times before giving up.

Next: The noise wakes Esty in her crib. Eliana wanders into the hallway. My mom heads upstairs to quiet them down. We all go to bed.

But not this time:

"Are you selling the house?" I ask.

Everyone freezes. They turn to stare at me.

Eitan shouts, "You're *what*?!"

Cue Esty crying upstairs.

Eliana calls, "Imma?"

Our parents look at each other. My mom turns to Avital: "Can you see to your sisters, please?"

Avital nods and runs upstairs as my parents lead me and Eitan back into the kitchen. Our father scans the mini meal we've started eating. He lifts the tray of food from the counter and brings it to the dining room, setting it down in the center of the table. My mom brings the challah and some leftover dips from Friday night, the brownies too. Eitan puts out cups and a half-finished bottle of seltzer. Soon the whole table's set. All leftovers and mismatched paper plates.

My dad and mom sit. Eitan and I sit. None of us has spoken a word since leaving the living room.

"Oh no!" my mom says, rising from the table seconds after sitting down. Avital steps into the dining room, one little sister in each arm. My mom reaches for them, takes them. And even though Esty and Eliana still have tears in their eyes, noses all snotty, both are already smiling.

"They didn't want to be left out of the fun," Avital explains.

"And who could blame them?" my mom says. She returns to her chair, Esty and Eliana planted on her lap, heads in the crooks of her neck.

Avital sits, looks down at her hands for a moment, and then over at me. "Cat's out of the bag, huh? How'd you find out?"

For a moment, I think of Finn, wonder what kind of excuse he would give. Something elaborate and convincing. And if it didn't work—he'd run the loop over again until it did. But I don't need anything like that. My dad looks at me, looks away. "Doesn't matter how you found out," he says to me. "We were going to tell you after the weekend."

"We wanted your bar mitzvah to be easy," my mom adds. "Simple."

Eitan turns toward my parents. "So it's true? You're selling the house?"

"Sold," my mom corrects, rubbing my dad's back. "We *sold* the house."

Abba sighs. "We really were going to tell you all after the bar mitzvah was done. It's the right thing for us, between rising costs and"—he pauses for a moment—"me losing my job."

Avital sits up straight. "That's why I started working too, Abba. To help."

Our dad looks around the table. Our mom holds his hand tight. For a second, Abba puffs his chest, lifts his head. Then he deflates. "I know that, Avital. And I'm so proud of you, in my own knucklehead backward way. I appreciate what you're trying to do. I've been . . . embarrassed. You shouldn't have to be responsible for us. It's the other way around."

Avital stands, steps over to our dad, wraps him in a hug. "We're responsible for each other," she says. "We're a family."

Avital retakes her seat. We're all quiet for another moment until I voice something that's been bothering me. Something else. "If things were bad, why did we even *have* a bar mitzvah? We could have saved the money. I didn't need any of this."

"Oh, Ez," my mom says, looking at me, then at my dad. Some small silent conversation passes between them. "Please don't think about this weekend like that. Things aren't *bad*. This is just life, with its ups and downs. As for the bar mitzvah, the community pitched in to help. The shul made all the food. Your uncle Chaim paid for the room at the Bergenville. We wanted you to have the best bar mitzvah you could have. One last special weekend in this amazing house that has given us so much."

All this time. Every argument. All the words unsaid.

My family—not ignoring me, not neglecting me. Protecting me. Wanting for me as much as they could give. Wanting *more*.

"Wait," Eliana says, chiming in for the first time. "We're moving?!"

It's hard not to smile at that, at how long it took five-year-old Eliana to understand what was happening. Then again, it took thirteen-year-old me much, much longer.

"Imma," Eliana croaks, blinking up at our mom's face, worry in her eyes. "Can I . . . can I bring my LEGO blocks?"

Our mom smiles and kisses Eliana on the top of her head. "Every last one."

"Maybe except for the spiky gems," Eitan suggests, rubbing his foot at the spot where he stepped on them last night.

"Oh, I wouldn't miss the gems," Avital agrees, leaning across the table to poke Eliana on the nose.

"Yeah!" Eliana agrees. "Good riddance!"

And now we're all smiling and laughing and just . . . sitting. Around our table. Together.

"Wait," Eitan says. "'One last special weekend'? When are we moving?"

"Truck comes on Thursday," Imma answers.

"*This* Thursday?" Eitan and Avital shout at the same time.

I groan to myself. *That's what all those boxes are for in the garage.*

"Don't worry," our dad says. "We'll do the move in phases. We should be able to start making small trips to the new house on Monday. And we'll have until the end of the month to close out here for good."

We sit with that for a while.

Monday. A whole new life begins on Monday. This is our last weekend in a house we've lived in for years, for what feels like forever, always. A wave of sadness trickles down from my head to my toes. Then a wave of relief: *Not* the last weekend. Not as long as Finn and I don't want it to be.

Eitan's head has been bent down at the table. When he looks up, there are tears in his eyes. I can't remember the last time I saw him cry.

"Are we going to be okay?" he asks, cheeks wet.

My dad smiles. A *real* smile. Full and warm. I can't remember the last time I saw that either. "We are going to be fine."

His eyes linger on my mom, Esty and Eliana asleep on her lap. On Avital and Eitan. On me.

"We have our health. Our new house is small but nice—we'll still have a roof over our heads. And we have each other. What else could we want?"

28

FINN

What I've done is wrong.

I know it's wrong.

But I didn't have a choice. I *don't* have a choice. I can't let time move forward. Not now. Not ever. Not after what I learned. Not after what I started to notice after I followed Avital to her job. And once my eyes were open, I noticed it everywhere. In the way my dad held my mom's hand, like the string of a balloon he was afraid might float away. In their whispers to each other when they thought I wasn't listening. In how she looked at me when she thought I was already asleep. All of it, right under my nose.

I lean my bike against the garage wall and make my

way through the mudroom. They're sitting at the kitchen island. Him, with a soggy bowl of cereal. Her, with a full mug of tea she's let cool. I didn't mean to stay out this late. I thought I could get the drive and come back without them noticing. I know I used to do it all the time—let them worry. Time will start over, I told myself. The loop will reset. But Ezra's right: We hurt people. Even if they forgot, even if it's all in the past, it wasn't right.

They stand and rush to me, hug me, yell at me.

"Where have you been?"

"Are you all right?"

"Why didn't you answer your phone?"

"Talk to us."

I know what to say. Exactly which words will send this loop into one of its many variations I haven't taken nearly enough advantage of: The Saturday night where we order takeout and do a thousand-piece puzzle. The Saturday night we flip through family photo albums until my dad falls asleep on the couch. The Saturday night where we put on a movie and make so much buttered popcorn that the lid pushes up and off the pot by itself. There might be a hundred different ways this night can go, a thousand. I want to live them all, collect every single version where we're here together, happy, as though everything is fine.

But everything isn't fine.

It never was.

"Why didn't you tell me?" I ask, my voice low.

They back up, give me space. I peer into my mom's face, searching it for signs that have been there the whole time—*every time*—but that I've been too distracted to see. "Why didn't you tell me you were sick?"

They look at each other, their faces scrunched into question marks. They're not sure what happens from here. For the first time in a long time, neither am I.

Tears well up in my father's eyes. He doesn't know what to say. My mom reaches out to him, squeezes his arm a bit before letting go. "Give me a few minutes with Finn, okay?"

My dad's eyes flit back and forth across her face, like the hand on a grandfather clock. One second, this way. One second, that way.

"Okay," he says, stepping away from her, kissing me on the top of the head, leaving us alone.

"Sit," my mom says gently, holding a hand toward the kitchen. Slowly, carefully, like any sudden movement might shatter glass, I sit where my father was sitting and watch as Mom floats about the kitchen. She removes two clean mugs from the cabinet, drops a new tea bag in each, pours us hot water from the kettle.

"Are you—?" I start.

But before I can ask anything, she slides a plastic bear across the countertop, raises an eyebrow, smiles. She says, "It's tea with honey, remember? Not honey with tea."

And even though she's said those words to me a thousand times—those exact silly nothing words—they feel completely different, completely new.

I drizzle a bit of honey into my mug and take a sip, shuddering at the bitter taste, ignoring an instinct to squeeze out the rest of the bear.

"You have questions," my mom finally says.

I'm not sure where to start. "You're sick?"

"I am. I have stage two thyroid cancer." She says it so simply, like it's a fact as ordinary and unsurprising as Earth spins round and round.

"What does that mean?" I ask.

"It means . . . that I have cells in my body that aren't behaving like they should. They're growing when they're not supposed to."

"Do you . . . do you *feel* sick?"

She shrugs. "Sometimes. I think so. To be honest, your father looks at me like I feel sicker than I do. I'm a little tired, sometimes a little hoarse. But I'm lucky. They caught it relatively early. The cancer doesn't appear to be overly aggressive. It hasn't spread beyond my thyroid." She points to her neck. "A part of the body in here." Then she takes a sip of her tea, smacks her lips, sighs. "What else?"

I have a thousand questions. A million. I try to rearrange them in order of importance, try to speak like I might only get so many words. "Will you get better?"

She nods. "I think so. I hope so."

"How?"

"Not sure yet. Surgery, probably. Medicine. Maybe radiation or chemotherapy. I have an oncology appointment on Tuesday. Same day me and your dad were planning on going to the car dealership to pick up a new lease. You can come with us if you want. Skip school. Ask the doctor all your questions."

"Okay," I say. "Yeah, I'll go."

Unless I don't. Unless I never do, because she never does. She says she's *lucky*. Says she has *hope*. But lots of people feel lucky, lots of people have hope. And not all of them are right. She can't know for sure. The only way to keep her safe is to keep her *here*, to keep her *now*, to keep us all from moving forward. Because if things go wrong, if the cancer gets worse—

She squeezes one of my hands with both of hers. They're warm from the tea, familiar from all the times she's squeezed before.

"I'll still be here tomorrow," she says, as though she can hear what I'm thinking.

I squeeze her hands back. "But not *every* tomorrow. Not every single one."

My mom smiles, wipes a few of my tears, puts her hands on my cheeks. "Oh, sweetie. There's nothing any of us can do about that."

29

EZRA

I guess you never know.

You can spend day after day—week after week, year after year—wanting one thing. But you never know when you might wake up one morning and want something else.

"Be back soon," I tell my family.

This time, they all look up from their places around Ballroom C.

"Need something?" my mom asks.

"Want me to come with you?" Eitan suggests.

I wave a hand. "Nah. I'll be right back. Seriously."

They smile and nod and give me thumbs up. My mom is tying decorations in a pattern I've never seen before. My dad and Avital are arranging the tables closer together than usual. Eitan's watching Esty and Eliana, playing keep-away with a loose streamer.

I step into the hallway and glance in the direction of Finn's party. The usual kids, the usual families. Only now, Finn is standing with his mom and dad, welcoming people inside. He sees me. Waits a beat. Lingers between his parents, watches them watch him.

"Give me a few?" Finn asks.

"Sure thing," his parents say. "Take your time."

He joins me in front of Ballroom B, halfway between his party and mine.

We're silent for a moment. Uneasy. We both start some sentence at the same time and don't finish it.

"I'm sorry," Finn says, holding out a fist, opening his palm. It's the drive. "I shouldn't have messed with it. I shouldn't have lied."

I take the drive in my hand, fidget with it between my fingers. "I'm sorry too. I shouldn't have said those things. I didn't mean them."

Finn shrugs. "Eh, yeah, you did. And I deserved it. You're right." He tilts his head back toward Ballroom A. "Even the kids who show up today wish they were someplace else. And maybe I did kind of like hanging out with you or whatever, having someone who liked hanging out with me too. Someone I *thought* liked hanging out with me." He pauses. "I really don't have any friends."

I kick his foot a little. "Yes, you do."

He smiles, blushes.

"And!" I add, trying to crack the awkwardness. "You'll be getting a new neighbor soon."

"For real?!"

"For real. My parents told me our new address. Walking distance from your house. We can hang out a ton after time goes back to normal."

Finn sighs. "About that. I am sorry I stole the drive. Sorry I snuck around. But . . . I did it because . . . because . . ."

I hold up a hand. "It's okay. You don't have to tell me."

Finn is still trying to get the words out. His family isn't moving. His dad didn't lose a job. Finn is worried about some other change. Some other reason to want things to stay the same.

"It's okay," I say again. "*Really.* I understand why you did it. I mean, not the specifics. But the point of it—I understand. I get it."

He blinks at me. "You do?"

"But we can't stay here forever," I say.

Finn turns toward his parents. "I know," he says. "Not forever. But not yet. Please, I'm not ready yet."

We listen to the booming music playing in Ballroom A. Somewhere inside Ballroom C, I recognize Eitan's footfalls, Eliana's laughter, Avital shouting, "Ezra! Where are you?"

"Finn?" I say.

He looks back at me.

"I'm not ready either."

"I don't understand," Dr. London says.

We're in her office, seated across her desk, drinking from the water she's set out for us.

"You want me to stop?"

I push the Faraday drive across the table. "Not *stop*. No. Just finish your work and then . . . wait."

She stares at us, mouth open.

"We want a little more time," I add. "That's all. A few loops maybe."

"Can you do that?" Finn asks. "Can you keep working, figure out how to make the antidote, and wait? That way, when we're ready, we can tell you, but for now . . ."

"For now," Dr. London finishes, "you *want* to be stuck. You both do."

"Yeah," I say. "Exactly."

"Not forever," Finn adds. "But for now. We know it seems strange. We've been in such a rush to get out of here. And we still want to do that. Get out. But—"

"Now we want to wait," I say, looking over at Finn. "We realized how much we have, here, now. How much things can change, even from one week to the next. I honestly can't believe how long it took for us to figure that out."

Something shifts in the room, something about Dr. London's energy changes. From across the table, she shuts her laptop, breathes in and out, in and out, tears swimming in her eyes.

"You okay, Doc?" Finn asks.

She nods. "I'm okay. I was just recalling the greatest paradox of them all."

"What's that?"

"How it takes using up so much time before any of us can appreciate what it's truly worth."

* 30 *

FINN

Ezra steps up to the mic.

"Go, Ezra!" Eitan cheers from their family table—Avital next to Eitan next to Esty next to Eliana. Ezra's mom and dad at the center. They break into applause.

The room erupts. Ezra's family. Ezra's friends.

I find a seat in back and take it all in. Why is this time loop different from all the others? Best I can tell, it's not, except for one thing: Ezra's dad and sister aren't arguing. They were the butterfly flapping its wings. One less fight and everything changes.

Ezra pauses for a moment to glance around Ballroom C, his eyes lingering on each face. Then he begins his speech. Something else that's new.

"Hi, everyone," he starts.

Quiet settles across the room.

Ezra smiles. "Thank you for coming."

More cheers. Whistles of approval. The room is rowdy. It's never rowdy. Rabbi Neumann starts banging on the surface of his table like a drum, leading the room in a Hebrew song I've never heard but which gets Ezra smiling even wider.

"But really," Ezra says, quieting the room again. "Thank you for coming. Have I ever thanked you before? *Really* thanked you? How many speeches have I given? How many weekends have I wasted? I'm sorry. I've been taking it all for granted. This community—you helped put the bar mitzvah together. My friends—you're always willing to drop everything for me on a dime. My family—"

Ezra wipes his eyes, pushes on. "All this time. Our last weekend in the house. And even if it wasn't. When did I last offer to watch Esty? Eliana, we haven't played together in ages. Eitan, why haven't I been joining you for basketball across the street?"

Eitan cups his hands around his mouth and shouts, "Because you stink!"

But it's a joke, and everyone knows it.

"Then it's time you teach me," Ezra says, laughing

along with the crowd. "And, Avital, you were always moving out this summer, and the best I can do is figure out how to spend five minutes with you in the rain? You're leaving. And you *are* my favorite big sister. We should be spending *all* the minutes together."

"Let's not push it!" Avital yells, but she's beaming, her eyes glassy.

"Abba, Imma," Ezra continues, "you do everything for me, and I've been in such a rush to grow up. It's so silly. Wanting to get away from the people who care about me the most."

Ezra stops, eyes the clock on the wall. "Our lives are going to change. Our lives were always going to change. Got to grow up some time. But I should have focused more on where I was."

Ezra spots me in the back of the room, begins talking directly to me like we're the only ones here. "This speech is so corny, isn't it? Thankfully, they won't remember a thing. But I guess, even if they could, I should say it anyway, right?" He turns back to his parents, his siblings, slight notes of confusion on their faces. "I love you very much. I'm going to keep saying it. I'm going to act like it."

I think about my own parents, only feet away. I'm going to act like it too.

Ezra glances again at the clock, then looks away.

"When I'm done up here," he says, "you're all going to cheer 'mazel tov.' You always cheer 'mazel tov.' It means *good luck*, right? Not *congratulations*. The words aren't about the past, they're about the future. And for the longest time, that's all I've been able to think about. But now—all I want is *this*." He smiles. "I can't believe how lucky I am, knowing that tomorrow will still be the same."

Ezra looks over at me again. "It can't last forever," he says. "We have to grow up sometime. But not yet."

"Not yet," I agree, whispering to myself, ready to wake up in my bed on Friday morning and do it all again.

Because it's 1:36 p.m.—and then it's 1:37.

★ 31 ★

EZRA

My last bar mitzvah went by too quick.

I hop off the podium, immediately find Finn in the crowd. He grabs me by my jacket lapel. I pull my black hat off my head, compress it to smithereens, toss it in the air like it's graduation day. We both start talking a mile a minute.

"What happened?"

"Is it over?"

"Did you do something?"

"Did *you*?"

Before we can get any further, someone juts out a hand for me to shake. It's Rabbi Alter—the *old* rabbi of our shul. "Mazel tov, Ezra. Just wonderful. Your leining, the speech. Everything."

"Um, thanks," I say. "I didn't realize you and Rabbi Neumann were both at shul this weekend."

"Rabbi *who*?" is all Rabbi Alter says, before my dad calls to him from across the room.

Finn stares at me, at a loss for words for maybe the first time in his entire life. I look at my family, everyone grinning, everyone getting along.

"Maybe . . . ," I start. "Was that a perfect loop?"

Finn laughs. "Definitely not. You've convinced me. No such thing."

"Then what?" I ask. "Where's Dr. London?"

We scan the room, peek our heads into the hallway. Andy Pauli is passing by, clipboard in hand.

"Hey, Andy," I say. He points at himself, half confused, half upset that we know his name.

"Can I help you?" he says.

"Is the conference keynote over yet? Can you ask Dr. London to meet us here when she's done?"

"Do I look like an errand boy to you?" he says.

"You look like a *concierge at large*," Finn replies.

Andy rolls his eyes and begins flipping the pages on his clipboard. "Attendee list," he explains. "Let's see, Lee,

Leighton, Loomis, Low." He looks up. "No Dr. London. Now if you'll excuse me."

And he marches down the hallway.

I'm trying to sort out whether Andy is messing with us. Time-loop villain or not, I wouldn't put it past him. Then—

"There!" Finn says, pointing toward the lobby, past the sign that reads, "THIS WAY TO EINSTEIN ROSEN EVENTS." But it's not just Dr. London. It's also—

"Rabbi Neumann?" I ask.

Our voices shouldn't have been loud enough. They both seem to hear anyway, turning toward us as they reach the main exit. They're standing together, smiling. Wordlessly, eyes on us the whole time, the two of them *link arms and skip through the lobby doors*, which, for a moment, appear as a shimmering rainbow portal.

No one else seems to notice.

Finn and I are frozen, staring, until he nudges me in the shoulder. "Told you there was a portal."

We look up at the clock on the wall, the second hand tick-tick-ticking each second gone.

"What now?" I ask as Finn's parents spot him in the hallway, wave him over.

Finn's party is already dying down, while mine is just getting going.

"Ezra?" It's Dovi calling my name. "Where's Ezra?"

"Go," Finn says. "I'll catch up with you. It's fine. Have fun."

He starts walking toward Ballroom A as a few kids leave without so much as a goodbye in his direction.

An idea pops into my head. "Stay, Finn, okay? Give me a second."

I find Shai, Dovi, and Menachem Mendel. "Hey, guys, help me with something?"

"For sure."

"What do you need?"

"Anything."

I smile, glad that—this time—all I'm asking for is help taking down a couple of fake walls. Me and Dovi shimmy loose the panels separating Ballrooms C and B. Shai and Menachem Mendel handle the line between Ballrooms B and A. Now it's one big party, and I'm only sad because it could have been this way all along.

My parents meet Finn's parents. My uncle Chaim and Finn's uncle Toby take turns playing music from the speakers.

Kailee Rodriguez walks up to Finn.

"You're still here," he points out, stating the obvious. "Thank you. I mean, I know your parents made you come and everything, but still. I'm sorry I've not been the best classmate in the world. But in case you hadn't heard, I'm a grown-up now. Much more mature. I'm gonna do better, you'll see."

Kailee backs up slow, the tiniest grin on her face. "Glad to hear it. And you're welcome. Come find me on Monday, okay? We can tell Lila and Ed that they missed the best party in the world."

Esty's asleep on Eitan. Avital's twirling Eliana on the dance floor. And I'm watching, trying to take it in, trying to imprint this memory on my brain. It's too important to forget, almost like every moment is a moment you can only live once.

"Well, now, young man," Mr. Bendish says, sidling up to me. "That was an enjoyable weekend."

I laugh. "Thanks."

"I've been meaning to apologize for being so critical about your Torah reading yesterday. You're decent. I was in a bad mood. Nothing to do with you, and nothing you could have done to change it."

"Oh, I know."

He ignores the comment, lifts his cane, and tilts it in Finn's direction. He's squeezed between his parents, group-hugging like only they can. "Two bar mitzvahs in the same hotel on the same day. Seems like a good sign."

"I guess it does."

"Now that it's over, what are you boys going to do with the rest of your lives?"

Finn catches my eye.

"It's a good question," I say, making my way back to the dance floor. "For now, I think we're just going to enjoy today."

★ ACKNOWLEDGMENTS ★

Back here again, eh? I'll keep it short this go-round, mostly because there really aren't words to describe how endlessly grateful I am for the privilege and joy of telling this kind of story, in this sort of way.

Thank you to my editor, Ben Rosenthal. I remember the first conversation we had about this idea. I am as thrilled to be at the end as I was to be at the beginning. And of course many thanks to everyone else at HarperCollins/Katherine Tegen Books—Kathryn Silsand, Mark Rifkin, Andrea Vandergrift, Celeste Knudsen, Annabelle Sinoff, Nicole Moulaison, Katie Boni, and Robby Imfeld—as well as cover illustrator Maeve Norton.

Thanks as well to my agent, Elana Roth Parker (and

the whole LDLA team). Way back when, in the before-times, if you'd have asked me what type of project/mashup I'd have hoped to work on together most, the answer would have come out looking something like this: Hadran alach, middle grade, v'hadrach alan.

There's always more. Thank you to all the friends, all the colleagues, all the family. If I keep thanking you over and over, it's only because you keep supporting me and encouraging me, no matter how many times I loop back to the start. Thanks, Tal, for all the days and years, even when they blur together. And Serena, Henry, and Micah. The greatest privilege and joy is waking up to you every morning (even when it's way too early), helping put you to bed every night (even when it's way too late), and doing it all over again the next day, and the next. It's not just kids like Finn and Ezra who have a hard time staying in the moment. It's grown-ups too. Maybe grown-ups most of all. For me, you try to take every day as it comes. For you, I'll do the same. And maybe we'll get to live at least some of our single premium life to its fullest.